Grimaulkin Redeemed

L. A. Jacob

Published by Paper Angel Press
paperangelpress.com

ISBN 978-1-949139-00-6 (Trade Paperback)

10 9 8 7 6 5 4 3 2 1

FIRST EDITION

Dedication

To Logan,
Your father would have been proud.

ONE

ALL SOULS'

I N A WEEK, MY BOYFRIEND SCOTT WOULD BE "AN ADULT." Two years after dropping out of the military academy, blowing off his family, and younger than me by six months, he would be perfectly legal to sleep with.

Also by the end of the week, Tyler would be out of our lives forever. Tyler, older than me by about five years, had celebrated his 23rd birthday with his head in the toilet bowl after way too much tequila.

However, on this night — which was All Hallow's Eve, or Samhain, or Halloween — Scott and I stayed at our sanctuary space: Scott's store. He wanted to be open late for the procrastinating Wiccans, and some of the stores in downtown had candy for kids in costume walking by. It was an attempt to try and drum up support for downtown.

We hadn't seen one kid yet, and it was an hour after sunset. I sat at the end of the glass counter while Scott sat behind the counter. We got caught kissing once and offended a customer, so now we kept our distance in the store when it was open.

"So the first thing you're going to do when Tyler leaves is walk around your apartment naked?" I asked him.

He chuckled. "I don't do that anyway."

"Why not?"

"Because you would've probably remote-viewed me."

I laughed. I took in his red hair and blue tank top that accented his abs.

He plucked a lollipop out of the bowl for the kids. It was the kind with chocolate in the middle.

"I think I'll be having these around for years."

"Give them to the customers when they buy something."

The door opened.

"Hey, Frank," said Scott.

"Hey," he said, and gave me a glare. "You do some weird shit recently?"

I touched my chest. "*Moi?*"

"My phone's been ringing off the hook."

I looked at Scott. Scott looked at the floor.

"No," I said to Frank. "I haven't done anything."

He frowned. "Must be the season." He took one of the lollipops.

"You have to say 'Trick or Treat'," said Scott.

Frank flipped him off. Scott chuckled.

"You have a lot of work?" I asked.

He unwrapped the lollipop and tossed the wrapper in the trashcan before answering. "I got one cheating wife, one missing person, and one dog-napping."

"Dog-napping?"

"Somebody obviously thinks I'm Ace Ventura."

"Did you take it?"

"Sure. You can help with that."

"I don't know —"

"They're bringing by something tomorrow with the dog hair on it."

I swallowed. "Frank, I don't know if I can do it."

"Why?"

I sighed. Scott gave me a little smile to reassure me.

"I'm on meds."

"What do you mean 'on meds'?"

I couldn't look at him. "I have a mental problem. They call it 'psychosis'."

"What's it really called?"

"Schizophrenia," I muttered.

Scott came over to me and put a hand on my shoulder.

"Why the hell are you taking meds for it?" Frank demanded.

"Because the things I saw were getting in the way of my life."

"What do the meds have to do with you not able to find a dog like you find people?"

"I can't do magic anymore." I looked up at him. "I tried. I really tried. I can't do anything anymore."

Scott said, "He had one foot in the other world, and one foot in this one. They gave him medicine so he could be fully in this one."

"Who gave you meds?"

"The Rosicrucians," I said. "The people who sent me to prison."

Frank stuck the lollipop in his mouth and sucked on it for a minute, thinking. "Why didn't you tell me?" he said around the lollipop.

"Because I thought you'd freak out."

Frank waved a hand. "I've dealt with schizophrenics off their meds before. Usually in the back of a police car."

"Ha, ha."

"I'm being honest. You don't seem typical."

"He's a textbook case," said Scott, squeezing my shoulder.

"When did you start the meds?"

"A few months ago," I said.

Frank took the lollipop out. "Well, this kind of puts a damper on things."

"I'm sorry. I'll do what I can. I need the money."

"Scott not paying you enough?"

"He's not paying me at all," I said. "I didn't think he needed to."

"What do you need the money for?"

"Things are getting cramped in the apartment. I've been there for six months. They want me out."

"That's why he's at the store so much," said Scott. "To give them some privacy."

Frank looked at me. "I'll see what I can do. I'll probably take you with me to the animal shelters or something."

"Thanks, Frank."

He saluted me with the lollipop. "Don't mention it. I gotta go clean the office. I'll see you tomorrow about noon."

"Okay."

He left the store. I let out a long breath.

"See?" said Scott, stepping away from me. "See, it wasn't that bad."

"He didn't ask me a ton of questions like you did."

"Because I didn't know anything about it. He's been a cop, so he probably had that kind of training."

"Schizophrenia with psychosis. I have to keep saying it to get it straight."

He went back to the counter and got a bottle of water. "What was worse: coming out or telling your sister?"

"She knew I was gay before I admitted it. This," I pointed to my head. "She never knew. I think that's why Dom wants me out. He doesn't trust me."

"He should do some research like I did. You're not a violent type."

"But I'm a textbook case?"

"Everything but the antisocial behavior. The article I read said that not everything is apparent."

I looked at him. "Have you noticed a difference?"

"You don't keep asking me to sleep with you."

I winked. "Biding my time."

"Until when?"

"Tyler goes home."

"Ohhhh, I see your ulterior motive."

We both laughed. I still did want to sleep with him, but I wanted to wait for just the right time. And in a week, if all my plans went the way I wanted, it would be exactly the right time.

No kids showed up, and neither did any late Wiccans. By eight, I begged Scott to close up, and he finally agreed. Scott brought me back to my apartment. I sat in the truck for a few minutes, looking up at the light in the window.

"At least there's no games on TV tonight." Dom was a big football fan, and it pissed him off a couple of days ago when he had to move from the big TV to the little one in their bedroom.

"That's good." Scott leaned over and gave me a kiss.

He hadn't offered — and I hadn't asked — to move into his place after Tyler left. I kept hoping every night he would ask me. But he probably wanted his privacy after Tyler left.

I bent my head and ducked out of the truck. Scott drove off down the street. I contemplated walking around the block a few times to give Dom and Evie some more private time. But it was getting chilly and I had no jacket.

Well, I thought. *I have to face it.* At least that's what the Confessor told me. I took the side door and stomped up the stairs, making noise that would make them aware I was coming back, just in case they were in the middle of anything.

I opened the door. Rufus stood there to greet me with a wide grin and a wagging tail. I peered inside. "Want me to take the dog out?"

"It's okay," said Dom from the couch. He was watching some sports show, and my heart sank. After I took my pills, in a half-hour I would pass out. He'd have to move to the bedroom, dislodging Evie from watching whatever she had on TV, and another quiet fight would ensue.

"I got some work," I said, hanging up my jacket.

Dom turned around. "You did?"

"Frank has a couple of cases."

Dom turned back to the TV, but not before I saw his look of disgust.

"What?" I said.

"Can't you get a steady job? Like, I don't know … McDonald's or something?"

"Are they going to hire someone out of prison with no work experience?"

"Don't put that down on the application."

"They'll need references. And I have all these appointments with —"

Dom switched off the TV, turned to face me fully. "Do you have any idea how much extra you're costing us?"

"I know. We already discussed this," I said, trying to keep my temper down. One thing the pills did was help with that. "Are we short again?"

"That's not the point. The point is that you're using schizophrenia as an excuse to not be able to work."

"What? What the hell makes you think that?"

Evie appeared in the bedroom doorway. "Dom, honey —"

"Don't 'Dom, honey' me. You know it's true. There's a lot of people who have what he has and can work."

"How long have they had it?" I asked. "I just started with the pills."

"Newest excuse," said Dom, getting up from the couch. "'Wait until the pills work.' 'Wait until I get a job.' Our lives are on hold because of you."

"I never stopped you from anything."

"You can't afford this place on your own if we move out."

"You want to move out?"

"We're looking for a two-bedroom," said Evie. She got a glare from Dom. Evie looked down.

"No, we're not," snapped Dom. "We are absolutely not."

"I'm trying," I said. "I can't do what I used to do."

"Yeah, no magic." He wiggled his fingers in my face.

I instantly reached out and grabbed his hand, squeezing it.

"Stop being a jerk," I said.

My voice carried an angry edge that I had perfected in prison but didn't find myself using very often in the outside world. Behind that voice was the obvious threat of pure violence.

Dom glared at me. This had been building up for a long time. I could see by his eyes that he was ready for a fight.

"Mikey! Dom! Mikey, let him go!"

I threw his hand down, letting it go. Evie's panicked voice caused me to blink first. Otherwise I would have punched Dom right in the face. Instead, I pushed by him to the bathroom, slamming shut the door.

I sighed, sat down on the toilet, gathering myself together. Maybe I should try getting a busboy job at the China Inn or a dishwasher or something else. I couldn't depend on Frank all the time. However, when he came through, the money was good.

At least I didn't have to worry about the pills. The Rosicrucians paid for those. I got up and opened the medicine cabinet. There sat my bottle of pills, on the top shelf. One every evening.

It killed me to take them.

I took down the bottle. Not for the first time did I think about flushing them down the toilet. I hadn't thought about taking them all — that wasn't my way.

Someone knocked on the door.

"Mikey?"

Evie.

I opened the bottle and looked at the pills remaining. I was doing this for Evie, for Scott, so that I could deal with them and with reality.

Damn, reality sucked.

"Are you okay in there?"

"Yeah," I said, and shook out one pill into my palm.

I popped it in my mouth, thinking yet again that my magic was gone because of modern medicine. I poured water in the glass and took a swig, swallowing the pill before I thought any more about it.

I opened the door.

Dom was gone. Evie stood in the doorway.

"You okay?" she asked me.

"Yeah." I smiled at her. "I have a case tomorrow with Frank."

"That's good," she said.

"I'll give you whatever I make. To help."

"It's okay. Dom's just upset because they let more people go at the paper. He said he'd make more money being the paper boy."

"Why doesn't he try for the *Journal*? Or writing for TV?"

"He's been trying to get in the *Journal* since he graduated. He's overqualified."

"Overqualified? Really?"

"He's got an Ivy League degree. Why pay for that when you can pay somebody from URI, or even RIC, a lot less?"

University of Rhode Island or Rhode Island College degrees were a dime a dozen in the state. Brown University, however, seemed to be more prestigious. I didn't even have a high school equivalent degree. Hell, I still didn't have a driver's license.

She gave me a hug. "I'll talk to him."

"No, you'll end up in one of those fights that you don't talk to each other for days." I stepped back from her. "I'll see what I can do. I'll talk to the Confessor. Maybe he can suggest something."

She caressed my face. "I know you're trying, Mikey. It's been hard for you. He doesn't understand."

I kissed her hand. "Love you, Evie."

She gave me a haunted smile, then went into the bedroom.

I lay on the couch, picked up my most recent book, and read it for the half hour until I felt it slip out of my hand.

The phone rang at four a.m. I should say: *my* phone rang at four a.m.

I clawed my way out of the dreamless sleep and reached for my cellular phone on the table. I fumbled it open and said, "This better be good."

"I'm downstairs," said Frank. "Get down here. Now."

The hell.

I hung up while Dom came out of the bedroom.

"What's going on?"

"Frank's downstairs." As I went to the bathroom, I realized that Frank never got up before sunrise. There was something important going on.

I left the bathroom and let Dom in. I pulled on some clothes. Evie waited in line for the bathroom, and I gave her a kiss on the cheek.

"Did you fight?" I asked.

"Go," she said, turning me to the door.

Dom came out and didn't say anything to Evie. That answered that question.

I took my key and left the house, with Rufus looking confused, since I always took him out before I left for the day. I bounded down the stairs and came out of the house into the dark. The light above the stairs was still on.

Frank sat in the car, drinking a coffee from a Styrofoam cup. I got in, lifting the door while I shut it.

"You ever going to get this fixed?"

"I have to do something to contribute to you building up your muscles. I got you tea."

I took the tea from the cup holder: black with two tea bags, just the way I liked it.

"What's going on?"

"Something happened in Providence overnight. Hotchkiss patched it through to us. They're holding the scene until we get there."

Frank sped through the near-empty streets until we got to North Main Street. We passed by a cemetery — a huge one, from what I could see from the road. Then he pulled in front of the cemetery gates, where a police car waited.

Frank rolled down the window. "Lieutenant Reilly called us."

The cop waved us by. Frank drove down a few paths, and I got thoroughly lost. This was a big cemetery, with tombstones probably older than the city itself.

He doubled back, and then said, "Ah—" and pointed the car in the direction where a group of police cars gathered. We ended up in a really, really old, but well-kept, section of the cemetery.

Someone lined the police tape between tombstones. A cop lifted the tape for us and pointed the flashlight on the ground. "Watch out for flat stones."

We walked carefully between the graves. I kept whispering "Sorry" to the residents as we crossed over graves to get to where the police stood around.

A handsome man in a short trench coat, with dark hair whipped back from his chiseled face, stepped forward with his hand out. "Bennett?"

"Yeah," he said, shaking the man's hand. "Reilly?"

"Yes." Reilly gave me the once-over. "You're the demon expert?"

"More or less," I said. "Mike."

He shook my hand. His grip was firm, but his hand was sweaty. "Come take a look at this."

Reilly walked over to the gathering of men. They parted and let me in.

A tombstone had toppled over. Two flashlights lit on the back of the stone. It was covered in dark blood that dripped over the sides. There was an awful lot of blood.

I swallowed, got closer. I could see something under the blood, a black mark. I squatted down and studied the mark, following it with my eyes.

The mark was a long triangle, with an "X" leading from the base, the cross of the "X" directly in the middle of the triangle. At the tip of the triangle was "V" that pierced the tip, and curved ends around the tip of the triangle.

It looked so familiar. I got up, walked around it, faced it so that the tip of the triangle pointed at me.

I jerked my head up as I recognized the sigil.

"Oh, my God," I muttered. I refrained myself from making the sign of the cross.

"What?" asked Reilly.

"Lucifer. His sigil is under the blood."

One of the cops snorted.

Reilly stuck his hands in his pockets. "Lucifer? Like Satan-Lucifer?"

"Yes."

"Is the blood used before or after the ritual?"

"During. If I remember the *Grimorum Verium*, you offer a sacrifice during the ritual for Lucifer to appear. But ..." I shivered. This was not good.

"But?"

"I don't know if he was just here for an appearance, or if they summoned him into a person."

I looked around. Any trace of a circle would be gone because of the cops. I got up. Maybe there would be some burnt grass from an attacked protective circle? That would be too easy.

"There's no circles that I can see," I continued. "No protective or holding circles. The summoner might have summoned Lucifer into himself, but, if he did that, Lucifer would burn him up from the inside." I looked directly at Reilly. "Maybe literally."

Some of the cops shifted from foot to foot, looking impatient or uncomfortable.

"Whose grave is this?" Reilly asked no one in particular.

"Benjamin Cushing, according to the layout," said a dark-haired man with glasses and in a suit, consulting a map. A patrolman held a flashlight over his shoulder. "Died in the 1700's."

"Great."

Reilly nodded to another man, and six people, four women and two men, came forward. They took out plastic bags, tweezers and cups, and went to work picking up things. I backed up. The cops dispersed. I went over to Frank, who stood off to the side.

Reilly came over to us, along with the man in the suit with the map. Reilly flipped open a notebook. "Tell me about the ritual."

I glanced beyond him to the area, where the people swarmed. "There's different ways of doing the ritual to summon a demon. What he did — they're usually men — was put the symbol on the stone and then make an offering with a prayer. I'd have to look up the exact prayer, because it's in Hebrew." Before the meds, I would have been able to recite the prayer from memory.

"I didn't see any angelic presences to restrain the demon. Usually a summoner will do that, because otherwise the demon can control the summoner."

"Can the demon control the summoner after the ritual?" asked the dark-haired man with Reilly.

I focused on him. I couldn't see him very clearly in the dark, but the sky started to get lighter with the sunrise. "Sure, if the summoner lets him."

"Can the summoner stop him?"

"Depending on how powerful the demon is when he crosses over, he can. Lucifer, you know, he's the most powerful demon in Hell and Earth."

"So it would have to take someone really powerful to control him?"

"The Archangel Michael is the only one who can control him." I motioned to the area. "I didn't see his sigil anywhere. Just Lucifer's and blood."

"Could someone have done something temporary?" asked Reilly.

"Like had the sigil on a cloth that they picked up?" asked the dark-haired man.

I tried to make the man out a little more. He believed me. He was following my discussion. *Did he know about magic?*

"They could do that."

"You said there were no circles," he continued. "Could those have been temporary, too?"

"It would take a lot to do that. You would need a silver or copper ring the size of a hula-hoop, at least, to keep a person in there for a protective circle. The summoning circle would have to be wide enough to hold that tombstone."

"Silver or copper?" asked Reilly.

"I doubt gold, but that, too."

One of the cops came over to us. "The guy from security said he has to go home."

Reilly looked at the man, who nodded. Reilly closed his notebook and said to me, "Be right back."

"Sure," I said, watching him leave.

I focused again on the man in front of me. I still couldn't see him clearly, but he was taller than me, broader than even Frank.

He took off his glasses and rubbed the lenses with a cloth that seemed to appear out of nowhere. "So there's no protective circle, there's a sigil of Lucifer, and probably the blood of a human or some sort of animal all over a man's tombstone. Tell me, what do you think happened?"

"I think someone's really pissed off and summoned Lucifer for revenge."

"Why revenge?"

"Why else would you summon a demon?"

"Power? Love? Control? Wealth? I can think of a few hundred reasons." He put his glasses back on. "Is that what you did? Revenge?"

Frank went rigid behind me. I never told him the reason I summoned demons. I didn't say anything. It's better to say nothing when faced with the truth.

"Mmmmhmm," said the man.

Although sometimes it means the truth is right.

He looked back at Reilly, returning to us. "He was smoking weed in his car," Reilly said, disgusted. "Didn't see a thing."

"Or he saw too much." The other man thumbed at me. "He thinks it's revenge."

"It's got to be more than that," said Reilly.

"It's definitely more than that."

Reilly said to me, "Any other ideas?"

"Um, no." Although if I could use magic on the blood, I might be able to see what happened.

The sky grew lighter. I could see the other man was white, his glasses wide and round. He had an oval face, with the beginning of a double chin. He wasn't thin, but he wasn't fat, either. Average weight and taller than most.

"Can you write up a typical ritual?" the dark-haired man asked me. "The steps, what happens when, what you expect?"

"Yeah, sure."

Reilly pulled out a business card and handed it to me. "Call me when you're done with it."

As they started walking away, Frank asked the other man, "I don't think we caught your name."

The dark-haired man turned to us. "Chevalier."

I couldn't see his eyes, but I knew what the word meant. *Knight.*

TWO

SPEAK OF THE DEVIL

"So mind telling me exactly what you summoned a demon for?" Frank drove me back to the house. We sat outside for a minute.

I sipped my tea to buy myself some time.

"I think I have a right to know if we're going to work together."

"Yeah," I said, holding the Styrofoam cup close to me. Dom and Evie's car still sat in the driveway. "I was beaten up in school. I summoned a demon to get back at the people who beat me up."

"Revenge."

"Yeah."

"I hope you're over that."

"Way over that," I said, more to reassure him than to believe it myself.

"Did anyone get hurt?"

I put my hand on the door handle. "Yes."

"How bad?"

"Pretty bad."

"Anyone die?"

I didn't look at him. "Yes."

I heard him hiss as he exhaled. "Does Scott know?"

"Yes."

Frank put the car in gear. "Get a couple hours' sleep before you come down to the office."

I turned to him. "You still want me to work with you?"

"As long as you keep taking the medicine."

I exited the car. He took off, leaving me standing there with the cup of tea. I heard the door open from the house behind me, and Dom came out with Rufus.

"I'll take him," I said, holding out my hand for the leash.

Dom handed it to me. "What happened?"

"Someone summoned a demon in the cemetery in Providence."

"Which cemetery?"

"The one on North Main Street."

"North Burial Ground. Do you know what happened?"

"Just someone knocked over a tombstone, drew sigils all over it, poured blood on it, and summoned a demon."

He looked like he was thinking. "A different demon than the one from Slater Park?"

"There's seventy-two named demons. And it was Halloween."

He looked pensive, ready to ask me more questions, I think. However, I took Rufus across the street to use the school parking lot as his personal toilet.

I drank the cooling tea as we walked along the tree line. I tried to remember the complete demon-summoning ritual to write down, but there were parts I didn't know. I didn't have a grimoire — a book of magic — to look it up. The Rosicrucians wouldn't let me keep my copy of the *Key of Solomon*. Besides, the ritual for Lucifer was in a different grimoire the Rosicrucians would never let me get my hands on. A copy of that grimoire probably sat in the Atheneum in Providence. In order to use that extensive library, I would have to surrender myself to be a Knight.

I didn't think they'd take me, now that I was medicated.

Yawning, I went back to the house in time to see Dom backing the car out of the driveway. Evie had gotten her ride to the school. The car roared; its muffler had been dislodged when I took it out the night I went out to hunt for my cousin Becky, and we didn't have the money to fix it. It already had an expired inspection sticker, so we were living on borrowed time with that car.

I took Frank's advice and snatched a two-hour nap. At nine, I got up to take chicken out to defrost for dinner. I grabbed my gym bag and headed downtown.

Before going to the gym, I went to the library. I smiled at Jessica and Lilly at the Pawtucket Library's front desk. Jessica collected my "mail" for me, while Lilly would give me the side-eye for no reason. I never took it personally. A young man pulled books from the returned pile, stacking them on a cart.

"Well, hello, there," I said to him, giving him a wide smile. He was a little heavy-set, younger than I was, maybe about fifteen or so. He jerked his head up at me, surprised that I was even talking to him. "You're new."

"Intern." He bent his head and ducked under the desk to get the books.

"What's your name?"

"Jared."

"I'm Mike. I live here."

"You live here?" Jared jerked his head up, his eyes wide.

"I come here often enough I might as well live here."

"Oh." He seemed to be confused or wary. He backed away and took the cart, pushing it around the desk.

"See you?"

"Uh huh." He went to the elevator with the cart.

Jessica watched the exchange, a patient smile on her face. I handed over my books. "What?"

"He's slow."

"Slow?"

She pointed at her head. "You know."

Was "*slow*" the new word for "*crazy*"?

I didn't say anything. I was going to go look for books, but changed my mind. I hitched up my gym bag and walked over to the door without saying "good bye".

I was angry and sad and disappointed at the same time. If Jessica knew about me, would she call me "slow"? Would she give me that patient, condescending smile, too?

"There you are."

I froze.

That voice. I had left behind that voice months ago. My legs felt like water. I looked to my right: I stood in front of the marble stairs of the old Pawtucket library entrance. I was still outside. Out of prison.

"Been looking for you, Grimaulkin."

The voice came from in front of me. I slowly turned to look ahead of me.

A bald man, about thirty years old or so, well-built and wearing a black leather biker jacket, torn up blue jeans, and low hiking boots, stood a couple of yards in front of me. His thumbs hooked around the belt loop of the jeans without a belt, which was common in prison.

He grinned at me like an old friend. He wasn't.

"Malachi," I said, keeping my voice flat so that it wouldn't betray the conflict in my chest.

He inclined his head, still grinning. "So how's it going?"

"Fine."

"Oh, come on. Aren't you glad to see me?"

"Not a bit."

He threw his head back and laughed. "I've repented."

"Right."

His crime was too heinous. At least that's what I heard in prison. I heard he was never going to get out. He was the leader of the group of Satanists in prison, a group of people who were picked up in the '90s.

"Look." He unzipped his jacket a little, tucked his hand under the neckline of his white t-shirt beneath, and pulled out a necklace: a gold cross on a thick length of chain.

"That doesn't mean anything."

He shrugged and put the chain back under his shirt. "Sorry you don't believe me. I was hoping we could get together. You know, smooth things out."

I held the gym bag across my body.

"There's a gym around here?"

"No. I carry my books in it."

"Where you heading now?"

I had to think fast. I glanced across the street. "Work," I said.

"When do you get off work? We could meet for coffee."

"No," I said. Again, I forced myself to stay flat.

"We could talk about your favorite subject."

He held his hand out, palm up. In the center of his palm, a burst of blue fire erupted upward, shining blue light on his face, making him look ghostly.

He had magic.

I didn't. My stomach dropped into my shoes.

"I have to go," I said, not keeping my voice flat, not bothering to hold back the fear.

I broke from his orbit, nearly dashed across the street without looking back.

I heard him yell after me, "I'll see you!"

I ran into the YMCA, slamming shut the door behind me. Rosie at the desk said, "You okay, Mike?"

I shook my head, running down the stairs to the locker room.

I didn't realize I was crying until my vision blurred when I got to the bottom of the stairs. I sat down on the bottom step and breathed, trying to calm myself the way I used to, but it turned into quiet sobs.

Bastard still scared me. I punched the wall with the side of my fist, angry with myself.

Why did they release him? Why did he look for me? What was he doing here? Why, why, why?

Whenever I found myself in this situation, what did I do in prison?

I lifted my head. *Exercise.*

I worked out with the weights and machines for two hours, and swam laps for another hour, to distract me from Malachi — and myself. Working out made me feel like I was accomplishing something. I could beat him in a fight. I had done it before.

After a shower, I got dressed and headed to Frank's office. I didn't even get to say "Hi" to him before someone knocked.

I could not believe the woman who came into Frank's office. She could have been a model. Wearing stilettos, a black one-piece mini-skirt, and a short ermine coat, the raven-haired beauty carried a black shoe box.

Frank almost leered at her. I wanted to slap sense into him. She did nothing for me, but she obviously dazzled him.

After pleasantries, he asked her, "What's your dog's name?"

"Expertise. He's a pure-bred poodle. He won awards." She sounded like she had a sixth-grade education, though. She thrust the box at Frank. "This is from his last cut."

"You keep the fur?" he asked, as he opened the box. A tuft of curly black fur sat against the edge.

"He was cut the day before. I had Margarite get it out of the vacuum cleaner." She bit her lip. "You can find him, can't you?"

"Where was he last seen?"

"At our house in Newport."

"What's the address?"

She gave it to him, and he wrote it down. "You checked the shelters?"

She looked horrified. "Nobody would bring Expertise to a *shelter*."

"You never know."

"He won *awards*."

"I know, but whoever took him might not know that." Frank smiled at her. "We'll find him."

She dipped her hand in her sequined purse and pulled out a large clutch wallet. She took out two one-hundred dollar bills and placed them on the desk. Now Frank's eyes did pop out of his head.

"Find him by Saturday. He has a show in New York on Sunday."

We had four days.

"We'll do what we can."

"If you find him by Saturday, I'll give you three times your normal fee."

A hundred and fifty dollars an hour?

Frank was definitely going to drop everything to find a black poodle. Maybe we'd get lucky and Expertise was shivering in the Newport animal shelter.

I doubted it.

Frank rose and escorted the lady out, then rushed back in, scooped up the money and said, "To the phone book."

He yanked the phone book off the shelf and started calling. I looked stupidly at the box of fur.

I touched the bit of fur and closed my eyes. I tried to feel that fire, the bit of magic in me that had kept me alive in the prison, even through the runes of deflection all over the place to stop magic from being used in the prison.

It wasn't magic in the prison, the Confessor had told me. My concentration was broken immediately.

Frank watched me while I opened my eyes. "Nothing?"

"Nothing," I said. "I'm worthless here."

"I'll make some calls. We'll go down to the shelters tomorrow."

"I have an appointment in the morning."

"An appointment? Doing what?"

"Need to talk to someone."

He tapped the receiver of the phone against his chin. "Call me when you're done."

"I have to write that ritual."

"You can use my typewriter." He pointed to an antique of a manual typewriter sitting dusty in the corner.

"I'll use Dom's computer."

"What's the matter with my typewriter?"

"Does it work?"

"Of course it works. No wires."

"I'll take my chances with the computer."

He turned the page in the phone book. "Suit yourself."

On the way home, I peeked in the White Raven, Scott's store.

"Hello, handsome," I said.

"Hello, yourself." He smiled at me as I stepped inside. "Where you going?"

"Home. I was going to make dinner as an apology for waking everyone up so early this morning."

"Oh?"

I told him what happened. I didn't tell him about Malachi. I was still working through that.

"Who in their right mind would summon Satan?" he asked in disbelief.

"Nobody." I leaned against the counter. "He's probably dead by now."

"God, I can't believe that. Worshipers of Satan."

I stepped away from the counter. "Oh, my God."

"What?"

I took out the card from the detective. "Can I use your phone?"

He handed me the cordless phone for the business.

"I didn't even think of it until you just said it."

"Said what?"

I dialed the number. It rang four times and then a woman picked up. "Homicide."

"Detective Reilly, please."

"I'll take a message." She sounded bored.

I gave her my name and number. "Tell him that it might be a Satanist who summoned Lucifer in the North Burial Ground last night."

She went silent. "Excuse me?"

I repeated myself. "Just tell him that."

"Ohhhhhkay."

I realized I sounded like a lunatic. *Well, I was one. Wasn't I?*

"Thank you." I hung up. I smiled at Scott. "That solves that."

"There's such things as Satanists?"

"I knew them in prison." I wondered … nah. *Nah.*

Malachi?

"You're thinking, Mike."

"Sorry, something happened earlier that makes things too coincidental." When Reilly called me back, I would tell him about Malachi. "I have an appointment tomorrow and I'm on a case."

"The dog-napping?"

"Yeah. We have to get him by Saturday."

"That's not much time."

"Frank's on it."

Scott nodded. The door opened and a man walked in, dressed in Goth clothes. Behind him followed a girl in Victorian dress.

I looked at Scott and rolled my eyes. "See you later," I said.

Scott turned to the two. "How can I assist you?"

I didn't wait to hear the answer.

I kept looking behind me, hoping Malachi wasn't following me. As I crossed the highway bridge in Pawtucket near the

Sunoco station, my phone rang in my pocket. I took it out and answered it.

"Mike, it's Reilly."

"Hello, Lieutenant."

"What's this about Satanists?"

"I was thinking that a Satanist might have done this. I happen to know one that just came into town."

"You make it sound like a cowboy riding in from the prairie."

"He's probably on a motorcycle," I said, remembering the biker jacket.

"What's his name?"

"I know him as Malachi. I don't know if that's his real name. He just got out of prison."

"What prison?"

"William F. Blackstone Prison in upstate New York."

"Never heard of it."

"Maybe your partner knows. He seems to know about magic."

Reilly paused as I crossed the street against the light, hoping no cars would come barreling down the small hill. It was notorious for cars to come right off the highway and do just that.

"We'll check it out," Reilly said. "So you think he might have summoned Lucifer?"

"He was a Satanist, though he claims to be reformed. I don't believe him."

"Were you a Satanist?"

"No, of course not." I'm a magician. I *was* a magician.

"How do you know him?"

"Didn't you look me up?"

"Should we?"

I sighed. "I was in the same prison."

"Uh huh," Reilly said. "What's this Malachi look like?"

I gave him a description. I looked around, to make sure that I wasn't being followed, and crossed the street.

"Okay. Did you write up that ritual yet?"

"Going to do it now."

"Call me when you're done. Talk to you later."

We hung up. I walked home a little faster.

When I got home, I saw the car in the driveway. Dom was home. I went upstairs to see Dom at the computer.

Maybe I should have used Frank's typewriter.

"Hey," I said, petting Rufus as I walked in.

"Hey," he said, staring intently at the computer screen. "They said there was vandalism at the North Burial Ground. That's all they're saying."

"It's okay. Mystery solved."

"Really?" He leaned back from the computer and studied me. "What happened?"

"Found the guy. They're probably on their way to arrest him now. But can I ask a favor?"

"Yeahhhhh?" He crossed his arms.

"I need to use your computer to write a report for the police."

He looked at the screen, biting the inside of his cheek. "Sure," he said finally, and finished whatever he was doing on the screen. "I'm going to pick up Evie anyway."

"Did you fight last night?"

He shrugged. "I'm going to apologize. It's not her fault, I guess."

"But it is mine." He and I exchanged places. "I'll work on getting a job."

Dom shrugged. I don't know if that meant "Don't worry about it" or "Whatever". He took the leash down and hooked it on Rufus, leading him out.

I opened Notepad and started writing the ritual. First: setting up the circles. I wrote, calling the quarters from memory, then charging the protective circle. I left space for drawing the sigils, but I only remembered a few, not the entire encased circle. I didn't remember all the angels, just Michael. I forgot the Holy Words around the edges, and some of the prayers. I wrote what was expected: the callings, the demands, and the possible purposes.

It was so hard without references. Before the meds, I would have known. But the meds blocked off some of my memory now — memory that Grimalkin would have supplied. Grimalkin was gone. Home.

The door opened and Evie came in, looking exhausted. Rufus followed her with Dom behind, shutting the door. I turned to smile at her.

"Hi, Evie."

"Hi, Mikey. What're you doing?"

"A report for the police."

"Oh." She looked at the kitchen and sighed.

"I'll take care of dinner as soon as I'm done here," I said. "Take a load off."

She let her book bag drop with a thud to the floor and shuffled to the bedroom. Dom followed her. I re-read what I wrote, then printed it. It came out to four pages.

"Okay, I'm done," I called, more for Dom's benefit.

I put the papers aside and went into the kitchen to start dinner: Chicken Parmesan that Scott told me how to make.

Evie came out after Don went back to the computer. She saw the papers and started reading them while I was cooking.

"Dom said this is about the vandalism in North Burial Ground last night."

"Yes."

"You think it was a ritual?"

"Yes. Oh, I have to write the sigils."

I dug out a pen from the junk drawer and reached for the papers. She handed them back to me and I drew the sigils in the areas I had left room for them.

She took the papers and looked again at the report. "You know, some of these are actually beautiful."

"They're fallen angels. They're meant to be pretty if you take them out of context."

"When do you need to get this back to them?"

"I'll call them after dinner."

I did just that. I left a message because Reilly was out. Maybe he was booking Malachi. I felt pretty proud of myself.

Yep. Mystery solved.

THREE

SEARCHING

I SAT ON THE PORCH STEPS, WAITING FOR MY RIDE. It was chilly, but not freezing yet; cloudy, like it was going to rain. I didn't bring our only umbrella with me, assuming I could catch a ride home from Frank later.

A black car slowed down in front of the house. That was my cue. I got up when it stopped, and took my time getting to it. I slowly pulled opened the door and got in.

"Hey, Ritter," I said, not looking at his eyes.

"Grimaulkin."

He wore his usual fedora and black suit. As he pulled away from the curb, he said, "I heard you had something to do with the vandalism at the cemetery on North Main Street."

"I didn't have anything to do with the vandalism. I was helping the police."

"That's what I meant."

"It didn't come out that way."

He said nothing as he took a left into a parking lot and did a U-turn in the lot. "I knew you had nothing to do with the actual vandalism," he said when he got back on the street. "You're not a Satanist."

"You know there's one running around out here, right?"

"Obviously."

"No, I mean from prison."

"Who's that?"

"Malachi."

"He's reformed."

"You believe that?"

"Yes. We believed you, didn't we?"

"You're not believing me now."

"You need to give people who have reformed a chance." He stopped at a light.

I crossed my arms. "He doesn't seem reformed. He searched for me."

"Did he attack you?"

"No. He was friendly."

"Then believe him."

"He was in prison for years. What made him change?"

"What makes anyone change, Grimaulkin? What made *you* change?"

I glared out the window. What made me decide to send Grimalkin home, to take the meds, to admit there was an issue with me, not an issue with the demons? I knew, but I wouldn't tell Ritter.

We drove to the East Side of Providence, toward the water. We ended up on Thayer Street, going all the way to the end. When we could go no further because of a "Do Not Enter" sign, he stopped, put the car in reverse and turned into a parking spot in front of a red house with a black door. He always was able to get this parking spot. Call it magic.

We got out of the car. I went up the six steps to the black door and opened it. I was in a hallway, at the end of which was a locked door and two other locked doors just beyond the stairs in front of me. A white door was on my left; a red door on my right. I opened the red door, holding it for Ritter.

That room was luxurious, with two plush couches and two winged-back chairs facing a painting of a lighthouse on the shore. There were no books or magazines in this waiting room, just gentle furnishings such as pillows and blankets, some modern art, and a couple of vases filled with fresh flowers scattered through the room.

Ritter sat on the couch and I took the chair, looking at the painting. He said it was a picture of Beavertail lighthouse in Jamestown. I tried to pick out the brush strokes of the painting.

To the right of the painting was another white door. It opened, and a man with dark hair stepped out. He was tall, muscular, and, to be honest, a real hottie if you were into older men. He nodded to Ritter.

"Come on in, Mike."

He was the only Rosicrucian to call me Mike.

I followed him into his office. When I first went to him, I could feel the runes come crashing down on me, diffusing my magic like it did in prison. Now with the medications in my system, I felt nothing different.

I sat on the couch across from him. Next to the couch was a nightstand with a clock and a box of tissues. The clock was for him to see how long I was taking and when to wrap up. The tissues were allegedly for me.

"How's your week been?" he asked me.

"Busy."

"How so?"

"Someone summoned Lucifer at the North Burial Ground."

"So that was the vandalism reported?"

"Yeah. They called Frank, who got a hold of me." I tilted my head. "Don't they call you guys when stuff like this happens?"

"Not always. How did you handle it?"

"I told them it was Lucifer. The detectives were named Reilly and Chevalier. Do you know them?"

"No, I don't."

"Well, they asked me to write up a typical ritual. I couldn't remember everything." I crossed my arms. "I hate that."

"Hate that you can't remember things?"

"Yes. Especially magic. It took me years to learn."

"In prison."

I looked down.

"Most of it you learned in prison."

"With Grimalkin."

He leaned back in his chair. "We've discussed Grimalkin."

"You say he's part of my imagination, my ..." I used air quotes, "'psychotic break'."

"He's not your imagination; he's a part of you. At some point, we need to integrate him into your psyche, not hide him behind medications. If I remember correctly, you were the one who wanted the medication."

"To get rid of Grimalkin and Belial and who knows who else."

"They're part of you, Mike. You still haven't told me why you wanted to get rid of him."

"I made him a promise. That was the quickest way I could think of."

"There's more than just a promise."

"You're reading my mind, aren't you?"

"I can't do that."

"Oh, excuse me — my *soul.*"

"This isn't about what I can and can't do."

"You're a Confessor. That's what you do."

"I'm a psychiatrist first, who happens to be a Confessor as needed."

"A psychiatrist without a name or a real office. You work out of your house."

"It's tax-deductible."

I laughed. He smiled.

"We always argue about this whenever I come here," I said. "You always say Grimalkin and Belial are parts of my psyche."

"Mike, you're a very intelligent young man. Brilliant, in fact. You know, be it subconsciously, that I'm right. I figure if I keep repeating myself that eventually you'll believe me."

"So I should stop taking the meds?"

"That's up to you. You're taking them voluntarily."

"What if I stop?"

"Your psychosis will most likely come back. You'll see things and hear voices again."

"And my magic?"

"Maybe it'll come back. I can't guarantee it."

"What do you mean about 'integrate'?"

"We work with the voices and what you see, and try to incorporate them within you. It's like taking what's on a floppy disk and putting it on a hard drive."

I looked at him blankly.

"Finding a spell and rewriting it in your own grimoire."

"Oh. It becomes mine."

"You got it."

"When the demons come back, I listen to them?"

"We will work together."

"You mean I have to see you more often?"

"Yes, or you may need to go in the hospital."

I stared at him, horrified. "Oh, no. No, I can't do that."

Hospital meant *insane asylum*, and I'd never get out.

He raised his hands. "I'll do what I can to avoid that, but if you're a danger to yourself or others, I might have to. Can you promise me, like you did the first time I saw you, that you won't harm anyone or yourself?"

I exhaled, not quite a sigh, because we went through this question enough times that it was old hat. "Yes, I promise."

He nodded. "So after helping the police, what do you plan on doing?"

"I have to catch a dog-napper."

"Dog-napper?"

"Frank has a case. He's going to animal shelters and I have to help find the dog by Saturday."

He risked a glance at the clock next to me. "You can cut out early if you want."

"Can I? I want to go help him." I really wanted to get out of there. We would go around and around in circles, talking about the same things.

"Sure. Same time Saturday?"

"Depends if we find the dog."

"Call Ritter the night before and let him know."

"Okay."

I got up. I stuffed my hands in my pockets as he escorted me to the door.

He said to Ritter, "He'll call you about Saturday."

"Right," Ritter said, standing up.

"Think about —"

I waved my hand at him and beelined to the door.

Ritter never asked me about my sessions, instead letting me stew in silence until I spoke. He was good about that, because a lot of times, I had to figure out what the Confessor meant to tell me — what I was meant to think about.

I let out a breath. I didn't tell the Confessor about Malachi, and he didn't ask. I concentrated on what I had found on the North Burial Ground, not what happened afterward.

Ritter usually took me out for breakfast, and that's where I opened up sometimes. He would sit and listen, sometimes add a few things here and there to get me to think more.

This time, though, I said, "Can you bring me by Frank's?"

"All right," he said.

He drove me back to downtown Pawtucket, dropping me off in front of Scott's store. Scott was inside with a customer. I would stop in the first chance I had.

I said goodbye to Ritter. "I'll call you Friday."

He nodded, and I shut the door.

I dashed upstairs to Frank's office. He wasn't there.

"Dammit," I whispered.

I pulled out my phone and called him. He didn't answer. I left him a message, hoping he'd pick it up, telling him that I was with Scott if he wanted to swing by and pick me up.

I walked down the stairs and out onto the sidewalk. Maybe I should have gone to breakfast, because I could smell fried food as the China Inn got ready for their lunch rush. I walked over to the glass windows in front of Scott's store, and paused.

A tall bald man with his back to me stood at the counter. Scott laughed at something he said.

No. No, please, no.

I stalked to the door and wrenched it open, not meaning to pull it so hard that the bell over it clanged loudly. Both of them turned in my direction.

I stood, steaming, in the doorway. I took two steps in, letting the door close on its own.

"Fancy seeing you here," said Malachi.

Scott looked from him to me. "You know each other?"

Don't you dare tell him, I wanted to say.

"Met in the same hotel once," said Malachi with a smile and a wink.

My hands, clenched into fists at my sides, hurt because I gripped them so tight.

"You come here often?"

"That's my boyfriend," I said. Maybe I snarled at him.

Malachi raised his hands. "I don't play for that team."

"Better not."

"Mike," Scott said quietly.

"No, I know when I'm not wanted." He smiled at Scott. "I'd like to get a reading. Can I make an appointment?"

"In about an hour?"

He looked at a silver watch on his wrist.

Probably stolen, I thought fleetingly.

"I'll be in the area. That would be great."

"I'll see you then."

He waved, reached out to pat my arm. I jerked back before he could touch me. He walked on by without stopping.

"Mike, what's wrong with you?" Scott asked as soon as the door closed.

"Don't be alone with him," I told Scott.

Scott crossed his arms. "Is he one of your old 'friends' from your past somewhere?"

"Yeah," I said. "But not a friend. He's dangerous."

What the hell was he doing out? Why didn't the Providence cops arrest him? And was Lucifer burning inside him?

My phone rang. I took it out of my pocket.

"Hello?"

"It's Reilly. You have that information?"

"Yes, but it's at my house. I'm not there right now."

"Can you get there and then can you follow us somewhere?"

"I don't have a car."

"Fine," he said, sounding disgusted. "I'll pick you up. Where are you?"

"Downtown Pawtucket, near China Inn. You know wh—"

"Be there in ten." He hung up.

"Gotta go," I said to Scott.

He nodded.

"Please be careful with him."

"Mike, we put up runes so that no one could harm me in here."

I didn't know if they would work anymore. Because I couldn't do magic anymore, did it mean that the magic I worked in the past no longer was effective? I left the store to wait at the corner.

They were there in less than ten minutes, in a brown Crown Victoria that had seen better days. Reilly was driving. I got in the back seat which didn't have a handle on the inside.

Chevalier was in the passenger side, wearing sunglasses as part of his uniform. He glanced back at me.

"Hey. Where are we headed?"

I gave them the address and then said, "I got a question for you."

"What's that?"

"Are you a Knight?"

He laughed while Reilly turned to look at him. "In shining armor?" Chevalier asked.

"You don't know what I'm talking about?"

"Can't say I do."

"Do the Rosicrucians ring a bell?"

He turned around to stare at me. "My father had something to do with them years ago."

"Is that like the Freemasons?" asked Reilly.

"He said it was."

"It's not," I said. "They're like the FBI and Corrections for the magical types."

"I looked into the prison," said Reilly. "It's not in the system."

"It's a magic prison."

Chevalier turned back to face the front of the car. "I have some contacts," he said. "I'll ask."

"Didn't you ask Malachi?"

"He checked out," said Reilly. "He was nowhere near here that night."

I frowned, sat back against the seat. He had something to do with it, I just knew it. He had to.

They eventually pulled in front of the apartment. I ran in, petting Rufus and apologizing that I would take him out when I got back. I grabbed the papers from the counter and ran back out.

I handed them to Chevalier when I got back in the car. He looked through them as I asked, "So where are we going?"

"Cranston," Reilly said.

I settled back for the ride. We took the highway to Route 10, then took the first exit. We drove past a large mill building, taking a couple of side streets. Police cars lined the side of the road in front of a condominium complex of four apartments in one building. All of the apartments looked the same: gray siding with red doors.

Police stood outside of one door; people gathered beyond the tape. A truck with the lettering of Medical Examiner's Office parked right on the lawn.

"Dammit," said Chevalier as he got out of the car before Reilly put it in park. He opened the back door for me. "Come on. Quick."

Reilly got out of the car and walked over to a man in a suit similar to the ones that Chevalier and Reily wore. Did all detectives go shopping at the same store? Chevalier started across the lawn and I jumped to follow.

"Did they take it away?"

"No," said the cop at the door. He stared at me. "You're bringing in a kid?"

Chevalier said nothing as he jerked his head inside.

I could smell it first, like someone had backed up a toilet in the apartment. Chevalier started up the stairs, and I followed. The smell was stronger; not only a sewer smell now, but something sweet, thick, and rotting. I opened my mouth to breathe and avoid the smell.

We went down the hallway to a room where people were gathered at its door and inside. Chevalier pushed his way through, and beckoned me to follow him.

They parted for me to come in. I saw the splash of blood on the wall and window opposite the door. My gaze traveled down to what lay in front of me.

On the bed lay a body that looked like its chest had exploded from the inside.

The combination of the smell and the scene forced bile to come right up. I whirled from the room, blindly running down the stairs and out the door to puke in the flower bed outside.

As I stood there, shaking, very glad that I hadn't had breakfast, Chevalier showed up. He waited until I collected myself.

"Did a demon do that?" he asked me while I still had my back to him.

I took a shuddering breath. I couldn't not see that scene in my mind.

He tapped me on the shoulder and handed me a wrapped piece of gum. I took it, not knowing what to do with it at first.

"Yeah," I finally said. I unwrapped the gum and popped it in my mouth. I slowly turned to him. "Yeah, a demon could do that."

"Lucifer?"

I almost swallowed the gum. "Definitely."

I walked out onto the lawn, wanting to get away from the smell, the sight — the whole scene. Reilly waited by the car.

"It was her," Chevalier said when we approached.

I almost lost it again. *The dead body was of a woman?* I wasn't about to go back and make sure.

"Okay," Reilly said. "You going to be okay, kid?"

I nodded. "Just take me home."

They did just that. In silence.

So I had nothing to distract me from the bloody body in the bed.

I tried a walking meditation that I had learned in prison, while Rufus dragged me up and down the side streets. Eventually, my mind's eye got used to the bloody scene and I could pick it apart.

Was there a splash of blood on the ceiling? Were her eyes open or closed? Her mouth was open in surprise, so her eyes must have been open. I didn't get to see if her heart was still in her chest: my memory didn't register it.

A woman summoned Lucifer? That wasn't impossible. There were some very dangerous female prisoners in Blackstone. There were even a couple of female Satanists under Malachi. I knew of only one female summoner, but I was more knowledgeable than her.

My phone rang while I was thinking.

"Hello?"

"Where the hell are you?" demanded Frank.

"I'm heading home with Rufus."

"I'm at Scott's. You said you'd be here. He said you left an hour ago."

"Providence Police called me."

"I need you to come with me to see some breeders. I need you to find the dogs while I distract them."

"Okay, meet me at the house."

I guided Rufus back to the house, made a bologna sandwich, and then carried it outside to see Frank parking in front. I jumped in his car.

"Didn't bring me one?"

"Didn't know you like bologna."

"I didn't eat lunch yet."

"Want me to go make you one?"

"We don't have time."

I split the sandwich into ragged halves and gave him one side.

"Not even with mustard," he complained, after taking a bite.

"Well, sorrrrry."

He held the sandwich and drove. "We're starting in Barrington and we'll move north."

He inhaled the sandwich by the time we got on the highway heading toward the Cape.

"What did Providence want?" he asked.

"They found who did the summoning. They wanted me to confirm it."

"Were you able to?"

"There was no denying it."

"Should I know?"

"You wouldn't want to."

He shrugged. "You'll be getting some money in a few months, then."

That was a positive. We soon ended up in Barrington, and he went down a few streets, following a map book. The street turned into a dirt road, with a good mile of meadows on either side of us before we got to a farmhouse.

"Are you kidding me?" I asked, as we bumped around in the car. I could hear the dogs barking.

"Gotta start somewhere." He pulled into a flat section of the meadow next to a barn and turned the car off. "Okay, you find the pens. I'll talk to the breeder."

I skulked away from him to the side of the barn, following the sound of the barking. I walked around the edge, to the door which was wide open. Inside I could see it was dim, and the barking was incessant and loud.

"Shut up!" yelled a woman's voice from inside the barn. I tried to see through the gloom, and could see pens, like chicken coops — wooden pens stacked one on top of the other, with wire covering the front.

The dogs quieted for a moment, then started up again. I must've been upwind of them or something. I went inside and the dogs went wild.

"Shut UP!"

A woman stood at the opposite end of the barn. She stomped over, carrying a sledgehammer. I could hear her boots slam the concrete.

I counted eighteen pens full of dogs, all of them the same square-headed breed. Boxers? Pit bulls? No poodles.

"Who are you?" the woman demanded of me. She had wild curly hair and a square face like the dogs.

I grinned stupidly. Best to act like the village idiot since she had a weapon.

"Get out of here."

"Puppy," I said, pointing to the dogs. "See the puppy."

"Get out." She raised the hammer.

I could have disarmed her, I suppose, but I cowered instead and ran.

Those poor dogs. I dashed back to the car and got in. The woman didn't chase me.

Frank came back to the car soon after, a man in a flannel shirt watching him warily as he climbed in.

"Found the dogs," I said quietly.

"No luck?"

"Nope. They looked like boxers."

"They're fighting dogs."

He pulled out of the parking spot, and I couldn't talk to him until we got back on level ground.

"The way they treat these dogs should be illegal."

"It is." He stopped to look up another address.

"Can't we do something about it?"

"Yep." He glanced in the mirrors as he pulled out of the dirt road. "When we're done with them, I'm going to report them all."

It was long after dark when Frank brought me home. We hit six illegal breeders, and he had reported them all to the state police. Now it was up to them, but if I had my way, I'd take care of them myself.

By the time we got to the last breeder, I was so angry at the condition of the animals, their treatment, and their "training" that I couldn't say anything to Frank on the way home. He was on the phone with the police as he drove, and the more he told them about the dogs, the angrier I got.

No luck in finding Expertise, though. I got out of the car and stood on the sidewalk as Frank drove away. I had to take a few calming breaths while I stared at the house, focusing on the light over the door. When I finally felt calm enough, I tromped upstairs.

I walked in the door and Dom accosted me with, "You left out the lunchmeat."

"Sorry," I said, trying not to look at him.

"It went bad."

"I said I'm sorry." I headed to the bathroom to escape.

"You don't care, do you? Since you don't have to pay for it."

By this time, Evie would normally come out of the bedroom to find out what was going on. "Where's Evie?"

"In case you didn't notice, she took the car and went to her mother's. Which you said you were going to go with her."

"I'm sorry. I forgot."

"You seem to be forgetting a lot of things lately."

"Must be the medications."

"Great excuse."

I put my hand on the bathroom handle, gripping it tightly.

"She made me stay here to make sure you were all right since you weren't answering your phone."

"I left it in the car. I was on a case."

"So now if she's broken down on the highway, it's your fault."

I opened the door to the bathroom and slammed it shut behind me.

"That's right, run away to your meds."

I did my libations as he yelled at the door.

"I think you're using this whole thing as an excuse to not get a real job. You weren't seeing things before. You didn't hear things before. You can't stand being on the outside. You like being in prison, I'll bet. Did you have a bunch of guys to —"

I threw open the door and glared at him. The look I gave him was the same I used in prison to great effect.

It was the "Don't mess with me or I'll kill you" look.

"I'm going to Scott's house."

"How are you going to get there, huh?"

I walked by him without touching him. "Walk." I took my key, wallet, phone and I stormed out.

I got a little less than halfway to Scott's house before the exhaustion hit me. All the adrenaline from the breeders to the confrontation with Dom faded. I should have stopped, turned around, and gone home. But, no, I'm too stubborn. I kept walking.

Scott was home, and so were the other people in his house, because all the lights blazed on the first and second floors. A total of eight people lived in those apartments. They were usually students at this time of year, and probably went to Brown, since it was right down Thayer.

I buzzed Scott's apartment. The audio box didn't work, or at least you could never hear what the person said, so he just buzzed me in. I stumbled upstairs.

He waited at the top of the stairs. "Hey, Mike. What brings you out?"

"Argument," I said.

"Dom again?"

"Yeah."

He stepped aside as I walked into his apartment. Tyler sprawled out on the couch.

"I thought you were leaving," I said.

"Tomorrow," he said with a smile. "Tomorrow bright and early. So glad to see you too."

I snorted.

"Want anything?" Scott asked, ever the good host.

"I'm starving."

"I have some soup."

"That's fine."

He started bustling around the kitchen. I followed him. "Can I ask a favor?"

"What?" he pulled down a can of soup from the upper cabinet and fished out a saucepan from the lower one.

"Can I stay over?"

"Where are you going to sleep?"

"On the floor. I don't want to go back to Dom and Evie tonight. Let them have some quiet time alone."

He plopped a big clump of something gray with darker gray bits out of the can and into the pan, like shaking jelly out of a jar. He got milk and poured some into the pan with it.

"You can sleep with me," he said.

I stared at him, as my whole body tingled. "Really?"

"No hanky panky."

"I would never."

He laughed. "Right."

"I'll even sleep with my clothes on."

"You don't have to do that."

"It'll keep me honest."

He stirred the concoction in the pan. It did not smell delicious. He placed a sleeve of saltines in front of me.

"All right," he said, after thinking about it. "So how did you and Frank do?"

"Didn't find him. Do you have any idea what people do to these dogs?"

"I can imagine."

He took the pan off the stove, and poured its contents into a bowl. He put the bowl in front of me. I stared down at the gray soup.

"What?" he asked.

"It looks like prison clam chowder."

"It's cream of mushroom."

I stuck my spoon in it and poured the liquid off of it. Some clumps plopped into the bowl with the gray milk. Maybe if I added the crackers, it would be better.

I ate a spoonful with some crackers. It was salty. I forced myself to eat it, even while it reminded me with every spoonful of the prison food and the prison itself.

"I can't." I pushed it away.

"Sorry," Scott said.

I munched on crackers instead. Tyler padded barefoot into the room.

"Don't like Scott's cooking?"

I pushed the bowl toward him. He shrugged, sat down, and ate it. I couldn't watch.

"Mike's staying with me tonight," said Scott.

"So if there's squeaking, don't knock?" asked Tyler with a smirk.

Scott blushed.

I said, "No, there won't be. Promise."

The thought was enticing — even exciting. But I was tired. It had been a really crappy day.

I filled up on crackers and water, while the two of them discussed the next morning. Tyler was leaving at the crack of dawn and going north, choosing to follow the Canadian highways to Toronto. I listened and yawned. The clock on the stove read 9:12.

Scott said, "You staying up, Tyler?"

"Nah, I think I'll crash."

"Sounds good," I said.

Tyler got up and washed his bowl as Scott put out the lights around the house before he headed to the bedroom. He stood in the doorway of his bedroom, waiting for me.

I jumped up and walked over to him. He led me into the bedroom, and I shut the door behind us.

Part of me wanted to ravish the poor guy. But the more rational part of me wanted to crawl into bed and sleep.

He climbed into bed, looking at me to see what I was going to do.

I was true to my word. I stayed in my clothes and climbed in next to him. However, I put my arms around him, and held him close.

As I drifted off, I had a nagging thought that I was missing something.

FOUR

GOOD FRIDAY

I HEARD A MUSIC ALARM GO OFF IN THE OTHER ROOM, tearing me out of sleep. Then the music stopped abruptly.

Scott, still in my arms, moaned and said, "No breakfast."

"Rise and shine, handsome," I purred in his ear.

He snuggled closer to me. "Do I have to?"

The knock on the door was painfully loud. "Hey, you decent?"

I let go of Scott as he called, "Just a second." He turned over to face me. "You okay?"

"Not comfortable sleeping in jeans."

He chuckled, planted a kiss on me. "Thanks. For doing that."

"Time's up!" yelled Tyler from the door, and he burst in. He stood inside, saying, "Oh, how cute you two are."

"Shut up," I snapped, getting out of the bed.

Scott got out of his side.

"You're still dressed? No fun?"

"Shut up, I said."

"Okay, okay, jeez." He raised his hands and backed out of the room.

I got to the bathroom first.

Tyler left without much fanfare about an hour later. At six, my phone rang. It was Evie.

"Mikey, are you okay?"

"I'm fine. Didn't your husband tell you where I was?"

"Yes, Dom told me. I … we need to talk. Okay?"

"I know," I said, my voice tinged with a little sadness that I didn't realize I put into it. *They're going to kick me out.*

"All of us. Tonight, okay?"

"Okay."

"I'll make your favorite."

"Not tuna casserole."

She laughed. "No. American Chop Suey."

"Not with ketchup, please." The prison ruined it that way every single time.

"No, not with ketchup."

As she hung up, I sighed. Scott asked what was wrong.

"We're going to have 'The Talk' tonight."

"Want me to go with you?"

"Why?"

"You might need a mediator."

"That's what Evie's for."

"You don't want to make her choose between you and her husband."

That was true. Who knew what she'd choose. Her psychotic brother or her steadfast husband? The scales were not tipped in my favor.

Scott took out a box of Lucky Charms. "Here. Eat these. Tyler left them. I hate them."

They tasted like I had poured sugar cubes into my bowl and added milk for texture.

"These'll give you a sugar rush," I said, finishing the bowl.

Scott was smart; he ate Special K with dried berries.

"Want more?"

"God, no —" Again, my phone rang. "What the hell?" The phone number was local, but I didn't know it.

"Happy Friday," said Reilly's voice after I answered. "Guess what?"

"Someone else is dead?"

"Been taking lessons from that PI, huh?"

I sat back, while Scott gave me a questioning look. "If it's like the other one —"

"Worse."

"I don't need to see it, do I?"

"No. Mind if we come over?"

"I'm not at home."

"You get around. Where do you want to meet?"

"I'm near Thayer."

He named a small but expensive coffee shop that was close to Scott's apartment. I agreed to meet him there.

I pushed away the mind's eye vision of the bloody scene I witnessed and successfully hidden for just under twenty-four hours.

Scott got his jacket. "Someone's dead?"

"Yeah, but there shouldn't be. She was already dead. I don't get it."

I explained to Scott what had happened yesterday after I left his store. I left out the fact I had puked over it.

Reilly's car was parked a couple of doors down from the coffee shop. We walked in and, instead of the usual crowd of students, there was hardly anyone in the shop. Reilly and Chevalier sat against the wall, huge white porcelain coffee mugs on the worn wooden table in front of them.

"Get you a tea?" Scott asked.

"Yeah, thanks." I threaded my way through empty tables to where they sat.

"Who's that?" asked Reilly, nodding in Scott's direction.

"My boyfriend," I said.

The two of them looked at each other. "Never would have guessed," said Reilly finally.

"Prison does that to you," Chevalier said, looking me over.

In this place, I could see the color of his eyes. They were a very light blue, almost, but not quite, gray.

I glared at him. "No. No, it doesn't." I yanked out a chair and dropped into it.

"Anyway," said Reilly. "We just came from a house on Blackstone Boulevard."

"Three people found dead," continued Chevalier. "And the family greyhound."

"Decapitated. Well, as best you can decapitate with what looked like a kitchen knife."

"One of the bodies had the Lucifer symbol carved on it."

"The father."

Scott arrived with the tea. I introduced him, and Scott shook hands with them.

"Should I sit over there?" He pointed to a distant table.

"Stay," said Reilly with a shrug. "As long as you don't go blab to the press."

"I won't."

Scott pulled out a chair and sat next to me. I was glad he did.

I sipped the tea. "Is anyone missing?"

"The son," said Chevalier. "Richard."

"How old is he?"

"Twenty-three."

I nodded. "So that's your bad guy."

"No kidding," said Reilly, giving me a *"no duh"* look. "Is he going to end up dead?"

"Or," asked Chevalier, "is this a separate case?"

"I wouldn't know."

Reilly drank his coffee down. "Well, at least this was good coffee." He started to get up.

"Wait, what do you want me to say?"

Chevalier got up as well. "Why would someone carve Lucifer's symbol on a body?"

"Possibly as a sacrifice. Maybe he heard about the other summoning and tried to do it himself. I really don't know."

"Are you saying there might be a copy cat in Providence?"

"I don't know. I really don't."

"C'mon," said Reilly. "I knew this was a waste."

They both walked around us and headed out the door. As they walked out, I saw something dark move out of the corner of my eye: a shadow. I turned to face it full on, but nothing was there. A trick of the light.

"Jerks," said Scott, taking Chevalier's place.

"I guess they won't need me anymore." Maybe I should have put them in touch with DeLuna.

I called Frank as we walked back to the apartment to get Scott's car so he could open the store. I heard barking behind his voice.

"Did you find him?"

"I'm at a breeder."

"Another one?"

"Legal, this time." I heard an electric doorbell and then no more barking. "I'm hitting the puppy mills."

"Do you need me?"

"Are you busy? I drove by the house, but you didn't come out."

"I'm with Scott."

"I'm in Rumford. I'll drive by and get you at the store before I go to Attleboro."

We went to the store. When I walked in, I smelled leather. That reminded me … "So what happened with Malachi?"

"Malachi?" He turned off the alarm.

"The guy I told you not to be alone with."

"Oh! Nothing. Nothing much."

He wasn't avoiding me, but he went to the back room to get his money out of the safe and load up the cash register.

"What did his cards say?"

"I don't remember."

I frowned as he got the store ready. He saw my face and said to me, "You know I don't remember what the cards say after I pack them away."

I could ask him to read mine, to see if Malachi and I were going to intersect again. I never asked him to do that, and he never offered. I remember when Aunt Jane tried to teach me how to read Tarot cards, I couldn't read well for myself, or for her, because she told me I was too close to the subject.

Maybe the same thing would happen to him with me. He wouldn't be able to read mine because we were too close.

"Did you like last night?"

He smiled and blushed. "Yeah."

"We can do that more often. And with less clothes."

"Maybe."

I saw the dark flash again. I turned to look, but again, nothing was there.

"Can you do me a favor?" he asked me.

"Sure."

"Can you get me a large orange juice from the Coffee Cup?" He pulled out a five from the register and handed it to me.

The Coffee Cup was a hole in the wall restaurant four doors down, past the China Inn and across from the jewelry shop.

"Yep. I'll be right back."

I left the store, and started walking down the hill to the restaurant. I got up to the door, and saw a sign, "Now Hiring". I went inside and placed my order.

As the waitress gave it to me, I asked, "What're you hiring for?"

"Cook's helper. Interested?"

"What do I have to do?"

"Prep work, mostly. Some plating."

"Plating?"

"Putting food on plates."

I chuckled. "Oh, that. I don't have any experience."

Said the person at the grill, "Then you'll be cheap." He turned and smiled at me. "Starts at six dollars."

"A day?" If I worked in the laundry at the prison it would be for three dollars a day; but they wouldn't let me because I was too young.

He laughed. "An hour. Five days a week. Saturdays. No Sundays."

"What are the hours?"

"Five to eleven in the morning."

Six hours. Five days a week. At six dollars an hour. That would be close to $200. A week.

"It's under the table."

"What's that mean?"

"Cash."

"When do you need someone?"

"Yesterday."

"I have to tie up a couple of loose ends, but maybe I can do it."

"If someone else comes in off the street, I'll hire him first, you know."

"I understand."

The cook nodded. I left the restaurant and walked up the hill toward the store.

Walking down the hill toward me was Malachi.

We both stopped about twenty yards away from each other. He came toward me first.

"Hey."

"Malachi," I said, again keeping my voice flat.

"You have a real nice boyfriend there, Grimaulkin," he said with a leer. "A shame if anything should happen to him."

I knew exactly what that meant. I remembered him saying the same thing in prison to someone I knew, who was involved with a female prisoner. I remembered the beating the girl got from the other female Satanists under his control.

I dropped the orange juice and ran at him.

He didn't expect that. When I grabbed him by the lapels of his leather jacket and whipped him into the parked car, his look of pure surprise was priceless.

He recovered quickly and broke my hold. He gave me a hard shove. I threw a right hook as I backed up. He got it right on the chin.

The pain in my hand exploded, as I hadn't bare-knuckle brawled with him, and he was taller with a longer reach. He grabbed me by the shirt, yanking me to the car, aiming to put my head through the driver's side window.

The car alarm was blaring, so when I hit the window it didn't get any louder. Luckily, my head didn't go through the window, but bounced off it. He got to the side of me and punched me solidly in the kidney. He kicked the back of my knee, and I buckled. Again, he gave me a shove to the ground, making sure I would hit it hard. I fell against the parking sign and slid down to the curb.

He didn't hit me anymore because someone held him back. Someone with red hair.

"Scott?" I asked, blinking.

Malachi shook Scott off, turned his back, and stormed through the small crowd that had gathered. I had to use the side of the car to try and get up. Scott helped me the rest of the way.

"Are you all right?"

"I think so."

I looked down at my hand. It hurt to close it. But I could move it, so nothing broken.

"Come on," he said, and guided me back to the store.

Wincing, I dropped into the seat at the end of the counter. I would have a bruise on my side. Scott went to his mini-fridge to get ice for my hand and my head.

"You're going to have a nasty lump on your head."

I let him wrap a towel with ice on my hand as I held a bag of peas on my head.

"Sorry about your orange juice."

"I didn't need it," he said. "What happened?"

"He said something that pissed me off."

Scott leaned against the counter. "Brought up the past?"

"You could say that."

"If he's going to be hanging around in this neighborhood, you have to get over what he did to you. You're different now. You went to prison, for God's sake."

"That's where he's from."

He paused for a minute. "Oh. Maybe you should talk to that person you see."

"The Confessor. Oh, crap!" I took out my phone.

Its battery was dead. I had to call Ritter. I didn't know his number, because it was a speed dial on my phone.

If I didn't take the meds, I would have known it.

If I didn't take the meds, I would have been able to fight back.

If I didn't take the meds, I would have used magic to kick Malachi's ass.

The black flash happened again. I didn't turn to look this time. It stayed in the corner of my eye. I watched it, a black blob at the left side of my vision. Then it sparkled red.

"What's wrong?" Scott asked.

"Nothing," I said, half-watching that black spot.

"What's wrong with your phone?"

"It's dead."

Then I saw Frank pull up in front of the store and I heard him beep.

"Don't worry about it," I said, and jumped up. I unwrapped my hand and handed the bag of peas back to Scott. "I'll be back. Don't let that man in."

"Mike —"

I gave him a quick kiss and ran out to get in Frank's car.

"Got in a fight?"

"Yeah, Frank."

He pulled away from the store. "Scott?"

"Over him."

"Defending his honor?"

I crossed my arms and glowered out the window.

"How chivalrous."

"Shut up, Frank."

He chuckled. "Okay, sorry. We're going to a place in Attleboro. The breeders usually let me check out the dogs, but there might be dogs somewhere else in the place."

"I thought you said they were legal breeders."

"Legal breeders, but they might have illegal studs."

He took the highway north. This place was at least better kept than the illegal places. The dogs' cages were clean, they looked well-fed, had all different types of dogs, but they were still in cages.

Seeing animals like this was making me sick.

However, I saw a teenage girl playing with a litter of Rottweiler puppies. That made me feel a little better.

I peered into one cage on the floor. The bulldog looking out at me looked so sad. I put my hand against the cage.

My hand went through the wire of the cage.

I jerked my hand back. Both the dog and I were shocked. I stared at my hand, my injured hand, and it wasn't swollen any more. I opened and closed it and I felt no pain.

"Mike, you ready?"

The dog watched me get up.

"Sorry," I said to the dog, and walked out with Frank.

"Next, Foxboro," he said, approaching his car.

"Frank, I … Do you have the dog's fur with you?"

"It's at the office, why?"

"Oh, nothing."

"You got an idea?"

"We can try it later."

"We're not going to get back until after dark again. I've got three places to go — the last being Worcester if we can beat the traffic."

"Tomorrow, then."

He was right. We didn't get back until seven. I was depressed and wanted to cuddle Rufus. I trudged up the stairs and opened the door.

Evie jumped off the couch, and Rufus ran up to me like an old friend. "Mikey, are you okay?"

"Yeah. My phone died."

She hugged me. "I thought you were mad at us because of what I said this morning."

"This morning …"

"We need to talk?"

"Oh, right."

Dom stood up and turned the TV off. He came into the kitchen and stood at the counter. The symbolism wasn't lost on me.

Scott was supposed to come with me. I had forgotten again. I sat in front of Dom, Evie to his right.

"Mikey, we were talking last night, and …" She looked at Dom.

"You want to kick me out," I said.

"No!" Evie looked horrified.

"No," said Dom, looking steadily at me. "We were thinking of buying a two-family house."

"You could have your own apartment," said Evie, taking Dom's hand.

"You'd have to pay rent, though."

"How much is the rent?" I asked.

"Depends on how much the mortgage is."

"We can work it out," Evie said, smiling. "What do you think?"

"I don't know. I was looking at a job. It's six dollars an hour."

"Doing what?"

"Cook's helper."

"You're better than that."

"Evie," said Dom. "Even McDonald's won't hire an ex-con."

He had to bring that up. To avoid glaring at him, I looked down at my healed hand.

"Can I think about it? You're not buying this house tomorrow, are you?"

"No," said Evie. "Of course not, we're just talking about it."

I scraped the chair backwards on the floor. "Okay. Will you excuse me? I'm ready to burst."

"Sure, sure," said Evie, watching me get up.

I went into the bathroom and did my business. I opened the medicine cabinet. I counted the pills. Eleven. Eleven days of bondage.

I dumped them in the toilet.

FIVE

FINDINGS

JUST BEFORE GOING TO BED, I CALLED RITTER and left a message for him to not pick me up on the next morning. I knew what was happening to me. It happened in prison, after about six months of being there.

The next morning, Saturday, I was up bright and early. I took Rufus out for his morning walk. Everything looked brighter. I remembered that today was Scott's birthday, and I remembered my plans. I grinned.

I couldn't concentrate and hold a hundred–and-ten-pound dog at bay. I did see and allow the black spot on the left side of my vision to grow.

If I forced it, the magic might not come.

When I got back, Dom was stumbling around, trying to wake up. The coffee pot brewed some strong dirty brown liquid that was their sustenance. I knew better than to talk to him, so I fed Rufus and silently made a couple of fried eggs and toast, sliding one over to Dom.

He grunted his appreciation, because he didn't have enough caffeine to form coherent words. We ate in silence, until half his coffee was gone.

"Coming with me to the Y?" he finally asked.

"Yeah, I'll do that."

"You don't have an appointment this morning?"

"With Frank. He's probably not around yet. I need to go to the library and check my mail."

"I'll drop you off there."

"It's right across the street. I can walk."

He waved a hand. "Yeah, right, whatever."

Without Dom noticing, I grabbed a spool of black thread from the junk drawer. As Dom parked the car downtown, Frank called my phone.

"Hey, I'm in the office."

"You're lucky, I just got to the Y. I'll be right down."

I grabbed my gym bag from the car, just in case I would get time to go to the Y.

"I might not be back tonight," I told Dom. "It's Scott's birthday."

"All right. We won't keep dinner for you." Then Dom winked at me. "Good luck."

I laughed.

When I got to Frank's office, he had the box on his desk.

"If you're going do anything," he said when I walked in. "You have to do it now."

"No pressure," I commented, and opened the box.

I took out the spool of thread and unrolled some string. I exhaled slowly, and centered myself. I tried to feel the magical fire within me. I took some of the fur, some thread, and braided them together. I didn't try to concentrate on what I was doing, I just let my hands work — let my hands weave the spell on their own, without me thinking about it.

Then it happened.

The magic burst from my stomach, and up into my heart. I gasped. I felt the magic flow from my heart down my arm, to the charm I wove, and it lit up with violet light — the color of my aura, my soul. It infused the charm: a three-inch long braid of thread and fur.

I closed my eyes, and could see nothing but darkness, with a small line of light below me. I was in a cellar somewhere, because the mold smell was horrible. I was scared, but didn't dare make any noise.

I forced myself to open my eyes. That had never happened before, that I got into the body of another creature and could sense what it sensed. Maybe because of my feelings for the dogs that I had seen, I opened myself up to empathizing with the animals.

Focusing on Frank, I said, "I can find him."

I picked up his street map book. I opened it and started on the first page: Providence. I held the charm over it, but nothing happened. I didn't feel anything, and the braid didn't move. I turned the page and did the same thing.

The map book was a set of street maps for the entire state of Rhode Island. I kept turning pages, waiting for something to happen: a sense or movement.

I got to Narragansett, and the braid twitched. "Where does our client live?"

"Newport."

"Show me where."

"You passed it."

I turned the page, still Narragansett, and the charm jumped. I felt the magic again, the fire, and I dragged the charm over the page. It twitched over Boon Street. I followed that street until it got to Central Street, and it thrashed on the page.

Frank stared at the charm. "I swear to God, Mike, that's freaky."

"The dog is there somewhere."

Frank got up. He put on his shoulder holster, then a jacket. "Let's go check it out."

"Do you think you'll need that?" I motioned to the gun.

"It's for show."

It was never for show.

Being that it was November, and long after the tourist season, we were the only car on Boon Street, approaching Central Street. Frank parked at the corner, on Boon.

"Well?"

I tossed the charm in the air. It flew in front of Frank, slammed against the closed driver's side window, then fell to the floor.

Frank and I looked out the window to the house across the street. A brown picket fence lined the property, large trees in front of the house faced onto Central Street. A circular driveway showcased the front of the house, a Jaguar parked in front of the garage.

Frank picked up the charm and handed it to me. "Keep a hold of that."

I shoved it in my pocket when we climbed out of the car. We both crossed the empty street and walked up the circular driveway to the front door.

I always let Frank do the talking. He rang the doorbell and looked around. The porch was cluttered with wicker chairs; a small table sat beside each of them. The Jaguar was parked next to a mobile home that didn't fit in the open garage.

The door opened, and a woman peered out through the screen door. She had an angular face, pinched almost, with no makeup, and her hair was tousled.

"Yes?"

"Yes, ma'am," and Frank flashed his PI badge. "My name is Frank Bennett and I'm looking for a large black poodle."

The woman slammed the door in his face. However, she looked shocked the moment she did it.

"Got it," said Frank with a grin. "Bet your cut she's calling the cops right now."

"Or she's hiding the dog."

"Go around the back. I'll wait for the cops here."

I followed the side of the house, away from the garage, to the back yard of the house. As soon as I turned the corner, I heard the rattle of a chain, and a German Shepard came running at me.

Without thinking, I made the motion for the shield I normally used. The animal hit the magic and bounced off, stunned. I was stunned, too.

I was back in the saddle.

The back door opened, and I saw the woman, wearing only a sundress and barefoot, backing out of the house, dragging something out. I dashed past the growling Shepard and approached the deck. I saw the black poodle, digging its paws into the floor, trying to stay in the house.

"I see you," I yelled.

The woman whirled. She let go of the dog, who bolted. The German Shepard intersected it, and the poodle body-slammed into him. The dogs tangled with each other. I reached down for the poodle's collar. The Shepard snapped at me, but I pulled my hand back.

Expertise got up, and I grabbed him by the collar. The woman decided to rush me and jumped on my back, pounding on me. She was nothing compared to Malachi.

She punched the side of my head, but it was a weak blow. I straightened up, trying to shrug her off while still holding onto the dog. The Shepard decided to get into the act and launched himself at both me and Expertise. He ended up sprawling on top of Expertise, his front paws on my chest. Most of the Shepard's weight was on the poodle, so I could still stand up straight and try to shake the woman off me.

I pulled Expertise toward me, but with the Shepard's weight, I couldn't get him to move. I twisted my body sideways to throw the woman off. The Shepard tried to gain traction and jump further at me.

The woman slid off and landed hard onto the grass. Someone pulled the Shepard away from me. I could see Frank yanking the dog's chain.

"Get off my property!" the woman screamed at us. "Or I'll call the police!"

"They're on their way," said Frank.

The Shepard growled at me, but didn't turn around to face Frank. I held Expertise's collar in a death grip. We all stood there for a minute, trying to figure out our next moves.

"Care to explain what you're doing with my dog?" asked Frank.

"It's not your dog," said the woman, getting up. She brushed the grass from her dress. "It's my husband's dog."

"It's not his dog, either."

"It sure doesn't belong to that bitch."

I pet the dog, but it seemed either too stupid to know what was going on, or on some serious drugs, because it didn't act nervous or scared. It kept staring at the German Shepard.

"Do you have papers to prove that?"

"I don't need to show you papers."

In my mind, I could hear that woman we worked for saying, "He won *awards*" in that high-falutin' accent.

The cops took their own sweet time. They parked on Boon Street and walked across the driveway to the back of the house, where we stood.

"Okay, what's going on?" one of the patrolmen asked.

Frank showed him his badge. "I'm working for a client and that's her dog."

"It's my dog," yelled the woman. "My husband gave it to me."

"Do you have proof?" asked one of the cops.

And it all came crashing down.

The dog didn't seem to want to hang his head out the window. Expertise and I sat in the back seat. He lay across my lap, his head on my thigh.

"I think something's wrong with this dog," I said. "He's too calm."

"It's bred that way."

We found our way to a house on the shore. I held the dog as we walked across a cobblestone driveway to the seven-foot tall mahogany double doors that served as the front door to a gargantuan house.

"Welcome to Gatsby's house," said Frank, as he rang the doorbell. A Westminster chime echoed throughout.

I got the reference. I'd read *The Great Gatsby* in prison six or seven times.

"Oh, boy," I said. "A butler, you think?"

"At least."

The door opened. A man in a dark suit and tie stood in the doorway. "Can I help you?"

"We're here to see Mrs. Burke." Frank motioned to me.

The man looked at me, then down at Expertise. "Of course." He stepped aside. "I'll go get her. Please come with me."

We followed him into the first room on the right. It looked like a room meant to hold people who didn't belong in the rest of the house. The items looked used and abused. Even the books on the shelves were best-seller hardbacks, throwaways. I took a seat on the uncomfortable-looking divan at the opposite end of the room, while Frank stood in its center.

Soon, the door opened, and the woman came in. She wore a red dress, low cut in the front, high-slit on the side, and silver high stilettos. She was meant to distract Frank.

He wasn't, I could tell by the cold look he gave her.

She glanced in my direction. I let go of the dog's collar. Expertise didn't move toward her. He just sat there.

"I've worked on this case exclusively since you gave it to me. A total of twenty-eight hours."

She nodded. She turned to the man who had escorted us in the room. "Get my checkbook."

The man left.

"Where did you find him?" she asked.

"Your ex-husband's house."

She frowned. "I'll bring charges against him."

"I would suggest you don't."

"Expertise was discussed during the divorce. I got the dog; he got the kids."

Wow, I thought. *A dog over her own kids.* Obviously her kids didn't win *awards*.

The man returned with the checkbook. She made out a check and handed it to Frank. He looked at the check, then at her.

"Thanks for the tip."

She nodded. "Thank you for finding him in time."

Frank beckoned at me. I gave the dog a last pat on the head, and got up to follow Frank.

The door shut behind us. We headed toward the front door, when I heard a yelp of pain.

I stopped short, and whirled around. The butler-guy was right behind me. Frank put a hand on my shoulder. "Mike, don't."

I pulled away from Frank and ran back to the room. I threw open the door in time to see the woman stepping on the dog's paw with one of her stiletto heels.

The magic and fury filled me instantly.

"Get away from him!" I yelled, and waved my hand sideways. She got knocked to the side, flying into a table and toppling over a Chinese vase. She fell in such a way that her skirt went very high up.

Her sharp stiletto broke off her sandal, landing straight up. In getting up, she brought her foot down right on it. It went through her foot, between the little bones, like a sharp knife through meat.

She screamed. In my opinion, Karma had been satisfied. Frank grabbed me by the shoulders and yanked me back.

"Idiot!" he said, as he dragged me outside. "You could have at least waited until I cashed the check!"

"We'll get our money," I said.

We got to the car. Frank drove at breakneck speed, almost running red lights. He had to get to the bank the check was drawn on, in downtown Newport, before it closed.

As I hung on for dear life, wondering if my magic would protect us if we got stopped, he ran another stop sign and took a hard left into the parking lot of the bank.

He jumped out of the car and literally ran to the door. He yanked on it, and it opened.

I sat in the car, letting out a breath I'd been holding. A few minutes later, he came out. He got in the car and turned to me. He held up a fat white envelope.

In the parking lot, he counted out the money, giving me an extra fifty dollars. "You earned it, kid."

I stared at the stack of twenties in my hand. Dom was going to be happy.

And I, for one, was happiest of all.

I walked into the store. Scott was taking care of a customer, so I moseyed on over to the herbs. They were discussing wands.

I half-listened to the conversation as I watched the black spot on the left side of my vision get larger, more defined. Two parts flowed from upper part of the dark blob, parts that seemed to wave like a flag.

The door chime rang. Scott stood alone now behind the counter.

"So how did you make out?"

I put my hand in my pocket and took out a pile of twenties.

"That's great!" He came around the counter and hugged me.

"We're going to celebrate. Call the best place you ever wanted to go to. It's your birthday today, and we're going to do it right."

"You'll have to dress up."

"You'll have to bring me to Wal-Mart." My last batch of nice clothes had gotten wrecked when I'd gotten shot.

"No. You'll need The Suit."

"And a tie?"

"And a tie." He grinned. "You want to do it right, don't you?"

"Will it cost me whatever I have?"

"No, not that bad, unless you order the aged steak."

"All right," I said. "I'd better get home."

"And I'll close up early. I'll pick you up at, say, seven?"

"Okay."

"I'll call in reservations."

I raised an eyebrow. "This is fancy."

He smiled. "It's somewhere I've always wanted to go."

I gave him a kiss, a preview of the evening's festivities.

I walked up the hill to the Y. Dom's car was still in the parking lot, and I found Dom in the office.

"Oh, hey," he said.

"I'm going to do a quick workout."

"I'll be done in an hour or so."

"Perfect."

I did the weights, concentrating on the reps. The black blob in the corner of my eye went away while I worked out. Yes, it was happening just like it did in prison. And when I walked into the locker room to change into my street clothes, it didn't surprise me to see an old friend standing at my locker.

"Hello, Grimalkin."

SIX

BREAK

G RIMALKIN RESTED HIS SHOULDER AGAINST THE LOCKER, his black skin darker than the navy blue lockers. His red horns curled back over his blood-red hair. He studied me with crimson eyes.

He was even more well-defined than I remembered. He still had the thickly muscled legs and cloven feet. He wore a red sash that covered his nether regions. That was new.

"I've missed you," I whispered, not knowing if anyone would walk in on me talking to what they would see as empty air.

He snorted, stood up straight. "We need each other, Master."

"They tell me you're part of me."

"What do you think?"

He never said "you". He had changed. Or I had changed him.

"Let's discuss it later. In private."

He closed his eyes, bowed his head, and faded away.

Everything was back the way it had been. Everything was where it belonged.

I changed into my street clothes, and went upstairs to get Dom. He waited for me in the lobby.

"Were you waiting long?" I asked him.

"No." He screwed his face up. "You didn't take a shower."

"I'm taking one at home. I'm taking Scott out tonight."

"How's that?"

"I got money." I showed him. "Don't worry, after dinner, I'll give you what I have left."

"I … I wasn't thinking … Okay, I *was* thinking about that."

I patted him on the shoulder. "I owe you big time."

We walked down to the car, while I looked around for Malachi. I was going to be ready for him this time. No such luck, though, as I got in the car.

"You okay?" Dom asked.

"Yeah."

"You seem nervous."

"Scott wants to go to a fancy place. With a suit and tie and everything."

"Uh oh. I know what that means."

"What?"

"You better get a good dessert afterward."

"Is that what they call it these days?"

He laughed.

Evie was home, and the house smelled of Pine-Sol, making Rufus sneeze. I took him out for some fresh air and private time.

"Grimalkin," I called, when I got to the school.

He appeared before me. Rufus ignored him and took a dump at his feet.

"The Confessor said we need to be integrated."

"Why?" Grimalkin asked.

"I don't know, really." I didn't.

He seemed to want to push it. Well, we'd have to see if Grimalkin appeared in the Confessor's office.

"What happened to you?"

"You did not banish me. You merely covered me."

"And Belial?"

"If you want him back, he will return."

"Belial's supposed to be part of me, too."

"How sure are you of that?" He came closer to me. "How sure are you, that the people who put you in jail, that they have your best interests at heart? Are you sure they want to help you?"

His vocabulary was different. Detailed. He had grown and was much smarter now. Although he practiced the spells I learned in prison with me, he never got beyond basic noun-verb sentence structure. Now he spoke like an adult.

"I chose the meds."

"Because Ritter told you they'd help. Would you trust your enemy to help you?"

I never saw Ritter as an enemy, but as a guy with a job to do.

"Why is he so concerned with you? Ever since you went into prison, he would guard you. Months would go by without him. Then he would show up for a week or more. Then disappear again."

Rufus started walking, so I let him drag me. Grimalkin followed me, still talking.

"Ask him. Ask him why he cares."

"Good point. What about the Confessor?"

"He's an enemy, too. They're all enemies. The Confessor, the Knight in the library — all of them. They're afraid of you."

"Afraid of me because I can do magic?"

"Yes."

"So can they."

"Yes. But you have the knowledge of an entire prison population."

I stopped short, turned to face him, but he was gone. *My God, he was right.*

Rufus tugged at me to go home.

Dom had to manipulate the tie around his own neck before placing it over my head and on my neck.

"This is special. You didn't wear a tie at my wedding," Evie said, looking me over.

"I feel like I'm choking."

"You're supposed to," said Dom. "Whoever invented the top button should be taken out and shot."

"Aw, you poor babies," said Evie. "Try wearing an underwire bra all day."

"No, thanks," I said. "Do I look okay?"

"You look very handsome."

I slipped into my loafers. "I'm going to wait outside."

"Try my coat on," said Dom, handing me a black trench coat. Although tight in the shoulders, it still fit. "Perfect."

"See you tomorrow!" called Evie, as I left the apartment.

I only hoped so.

I stood at the fence, waiting for Scott to arrive. Being alone now, just waiting, I thought about what Grimalkin said. *Were the Rosicrucians my enemies?*

When I was first put in prison, I hated the Rosicrucians. They pulled rules on me that I had never known. They killed Aunt Jane. When they let me go, I thought I was free of them. Then Ritter showed up to make sure I was going to be a good boy. He acted so concerned. He talked me into using meds.

It was their fault I lost my magic. That's what they wanted, wasn't it? For me to lose my magic and be normal. Easy to control.

"No more," I said out loud.

Good, said Grimalkin's voice in my mind.

Scott pulled up. I walked up to the truck and opened the door. The dome light shined on him. He wore a dark suit and tie as well. He smiled at me.

"You look nice," he said.

"So do you." I climbed in. "Where is this place?"

"Downtown. Valet parking and everything."

"Oh, God."

We ended up across from the train station, near Kennedy Plaza, at a place called The Capital Grille. The building didn't look that impressive. Scott gave the keys to the valet and walked around the truck to me.

"It looks like a school."

"Wait," he said, and we walked in together. He took off his coat, handing it over a counter to a woman in a closet. I did the same thing and got a ticket.

The host looked us over, then looked beyond us, probably for our parents. He focused on me, because I looked older than Scott. "Do you have a reservation?"

"Scott Angrier," said Scott. "For two."

The host passed us off to a seater, who brought us to a nice table near the windows. Scott sat down. I just followed his motions. I looked at all the utensils on the linen tablecloth.

"Shall I get you a drink?" asked the seater.

"Just a Coke," said Scott.

"Same thing," I said.

He nodded. "Your server will be here in a few moments."

"Thank you," said Scott, and turned his attention to the menu.

I opened it up looking for the specials. With the prices here, there didn't seem to be any.

"Scott, the cheapest thing on the menu is thirty dollars," I said.

"I can cover it if you didn't bring enough."

"I brought enough," I said.

I looked around the place. We were the youngest diners here. Everyone else was so well-dressed: the women in dresses, men in suits — at the very least with jackets; most men with ties.

The server who brought our drinks wore a goatee, a crisp white shirt, a black bow tie, black pants, and was damn cute.

"Hello," he said with a genuine smile.

I could tell immediately that he was gay. And I think he could tell we were, too.

"We'll have the oysters to start," said Scott.

"Very good." The server left us.

"Ever have oysters?" Scott asked me.

"Can't say I have."

"They're an aphrodisiac."

"Like I need that."

He blushed.

I looked for something simple. They didn't have anything like Veal Parmesan.

"Scott, what the hell is this?"

"Do you want seafood, chicken, beef, lamb?"

"Beef." Better to stick with something I knew.

He looked at the menu. "Got it. I'll order for you."

The server returned a short time later with the oysters and a sauce with onions in it. Scott ordered something called Kobe steak for me and a tenderloin with lobster for him.

Scott took one of the oysters, poured some of the sauce on it, and slid the oyster meat into his mouth.

"Oh. Oh, my God." He closed his eyes in pleasure.

I tried to do the same thing, but it was a little awkward and I dribbled some down my chin. It was slimy, salty, sweet with the sauce, and chewy. I didn't want another one, but I ate two more. If it was an aphrodisiac, I didn't want him to get all the fun.

The dinners arrived, and I was disappointed. Kobe steak was a cube about the size of two decks of playing cards, with *au gratin* potatoes on the side and a pretty piece of rosemary. Scott's plate was also a tiny bit of steak with a lobster tail and drawn butter along with sautéed wild mushrooms.

"You're kidding me, right?"

He pointed. "Try it. A little bite at first. You'll love it."

I cut a piece and popped it in my mouth.

My God. It melted like butter.

"See?" Scott said with a chuckle.

It was like the finest chocolate for steak.

I savored each bite, and was sad when I finished it. It might not have been enough to satisfy me, but I bet I would never have another cut of beef that good again.

I was high and happy, as I crossed my utensils on the plate. "I'll be right back," I said.

"Bathrooms are near the coat room."

"Thanks."

I passed by our server, who smiled and gave me a thumb's up. I got to the bathroom and did my business.

Someone came in behind me as I washed my hands. He stood behind me. He was an older man, white hair, chiseled features, taller than me. He stood close enough to me that I could smell his cologne.

"Where's your parents?" he asked me.

"New Haven," I replied, looking at him through the mirror.

He put his hands on my shoulders.

Oh, no, you don't —

I ducked my head and water exploded upward from the sink, splashing him in the face. He sputtered and stepped away, wiping his face.

The water from the spigot spat out sideways and soaked the front of his gray pants. I ran out of the bathroom before he could see me.

The coat check woman saw me run out. She tilted her head, curious. I shook mine and straightened out my coat before walking calmly back to the table.

The bill was there. I picked it up and my eyes almost popped out of my head. It was almost the same as the rent Dom and Evie paid every week.

I left a good tip — the server was worth it. We claimed our coats, and waited for the valet to get the truck.

The man with white hair showed up behind me. He still had a stain on the front of his pants. He was with a pretty older lady. The man gave me a dirty look.

I smiled, put my arm around Scott's waist. Scott turned his head to look up at me. Then the truck arrived. Scott tipped the valet and we got in.

"What was that all about?"

"Oh, nothing," I said. "Nothing at all."

We drove back to his apartment. I had loosened the tie and the top button by the time we got there.

He parked the truck a couple of doors down from the apartment. I took his hand as we walked back to his apartment.

"So," I said.

"So," he replied.

"Hm."

"What?"

"Happy birthday?"

He leaned into me as we walked. "Thank you."

We headed to his apartment, up the stairs. As we climbed the stairs, I felt myself getting more and more warm and nervous. He took forever to unlock the door.

We went inside. He took off his jacket and carried it into the kitchen, draping it on a chair. I took off my coat and jacket and did the same thing.

"So," he said.

"So."

He grinned at me, grabbed my tie, and pulled me toward the bedroom.

The rest is none of your business.

SEVEN

MAGIC WITHOUT ME

THE SUN CREATED AN AURA AROUND MY BOYFRIEND as he stood near the window in front of the stove, scrambling eggs. I rested my head on my hands and stared at him — at every inch of him that I had explored the night before.

"What's with the goofy grin?" Scott asked as he spooned out some eggs onto a plate.

"I have a goofy grin?" I couldn't help it. This was bliss.

With a chuckle, he said, "Yeah."

"I'll try and act serious."

"No, don't." He handed over the plate of eggs with sausage patties.

"So what are we doing today?"

"We?" He looked around the apartment. "I was planning on cleaning the place up."

"I can help with that."

"You'll do anything to stay here."

"I'm that obvious?"

"Oh, yes."

Later, I tackled the dishes as Scott went into the living room, tearing apart the couch where Tyler slept for all that time. I rinsed a plate and my phone rang.

"For God's sake." I answered the buzzing device. "What?"

"Did you see the paper this morning?" asked Reilly. He sounded pissed.

"Uh, no."

"Go get it." He hung up.

I stared at the phone. I called to Scott, "Scott, do you get the Sunday paper?"

"No, why?"

"Reilly just called and told me to pick up the paper."

Scott came into the kitchen. "We can get it later."

"He sounded mad. Something about the murder must be in it."

Scott looked out the window. "I'll go get it."

"I'll finish these dishes."

He grabbed his wallet and went out. I thought about what could have gotten Reilly so mad. I didn't talk to anyone but Scott about the murders.

"Mike?" Scott called when he came in. "You'd better look at this."

I dried my hands and walked over to him as he headed into the kitchen. He bumped into me. Then he handed me the paper.

I saw the picture: a fancy house, and a happy family portrait superimposed on it. The headline: "Satanist Kills Family Then Self."

"Oh, shit," I whispered.

I skimmed the article. The teen boy in the picture "bludgeoned" his family to death on the east side of Providence, He was found dead the next day in Riverside with a .45 in his mouth. The article went into details that I didn't even know.

I called Reilly. "I saw it."

"So are you the unnamed source?"

"No, of course not."

"What about the boyfriend?"

"He's not, either." I knew Scott. He would never tell. "I swear. I didn't know half this stuff."

"An unnamed source isn't always the same source for the entire story."

"Reilly, I swear to God. I didn't talk about this to anyone."

He sighed.

"Listen," I said. "If you need any help —"

"Yeah, right."

"I mean it. I can help you."

"We'll call you." He hung up.

Scott opened the paper to read the entire story. "Wow, this reporter's going to start a panic."

"I still can't believe Malachi has nothing to do with this." I heard his voice in my mind: *A shame if something happened to him.*

Scott's phone rang. He walked over to the cradle and picked up the cordless phone.

"Hello? Hi, Evie. Yes, he's here. Sure." He handed the phone to me.

"Hi, Mikey," she said. "Do you want me to pick you up on the way to Mom and Dad's?"

There went staying with Scott for the entire day. *Unless …*

"What if Scott comes?"

Scott turned to look at me.

Evie hummed for a minute. "Are you sure? Are you ready for that?"

"Yes. Yes, I'm ready for that." I was ready to stand on the roof and announce to the world that had met the man of my dreams.

Scott raised his hands. "I'm not."

"Maybe you should tell them first before you bring him over?" Evie asked.

I suppose it wouldn't be fair to Scott if I showed up at my parent's house and said, "Hi, I'm gay, and here's my boyfriend." Maybe I should break it down in small pieces.

"It's called coming out," I said.

"They don't *know*?" Scott blurted.

"The topic never came up."

"You should tell them first," came Evie's voice from the phone.

"Okay, okay. Yeah, pick me up. When will you be here?"

"In ten minutes."

I was in my suit pants and a white t-shirt. "Bring me a change of clothes?"

"See you in fifteen, then."

After I hung up, I said to Scott, "I have to go to my parent's."

"I figured that out."

"I would have brought you, but ..."

He took my hands. "There's plenty of time for that."

I looked down at his hands. I squeezed them. "I suppose."

When Evie arrived, I ducked into the cellar and changed clothes really quick. She had even brought my sneakers. Scott gave me a wooden hanger for my suit. He never had wire hangers.

I kissed Scott goodbye, and climbed into the back seat of the Camry. The muffler rattled under me. We normally couldn't talk, and the radio was on full blast because of the muffler.

Dom turned to me. "Score?"

My face got hot.

"Awright!" he cried, holding his hand up for a high-five.

"Dom!" Evie grabbed his hand and yanked it down.

He laughed.

Evie turned down the radio and said to me. "So what are you going to say?"

"To Mom and Dad?"

"Maybe Mom. I don't know how Dad will take it."

"I don't care how Dad will take it."

"You two just started talking again. Don't ruin it."

"That's because baseball season is over and he had nothing else to do."

"You also weren't so hot-tempered," Dom butted in.

I realized that I had to pay attention to that. They thought I was still on the medicine. I would have to work on my temper. It was something I had to work on when I first started seeing the Confessor, anyway.

"Sensitive," said Evie to Dom. "The word you want is 'sensitive'." She turned back to me. "So?"

"I don't know, yet, Evie. I'll just tell them, I guess."

Evie put the radio back up. I needed to do something about this car. Which reminded me …

"Hey," I said, sticking my hand in my pocket. I pulled out what money I had left. "Here."

Evie glanced at Dom, who only nodded. She took the money from me. "Thank you, Mike. Really."

"For what you've done for me, it's the least I can do."

Dom kept his eyes on the road, but I could read his mind like a thought-bubble over his head. *About time.*

We got off the highway and headed into the suburbs, then the condo area my parents lived in. I came usually only to see my mother. Like Evie said, my father and I started talking to each other only recently. He didn't like the fact that I was alive and his eldest son Philip was dead. No one in the family knew that Phil died because I wanted him to.

I unfolded out of the back of the Camry and followed Evie to the back of the house. The summer deck furniture had been packed away, the grill covered. Evie knocked on the sliding glass door. My mother came and opened it.

Immediately, I was assaulted by the smell of her cooking. It was barbecue. Not exactly my favorite, but it was free food. I never complained.

She hugged each of us as we walked in.

"How are you?" she asked me. "I haven't seen you in a couple of weeks."

"Sorry. Got busy."

She headed into the kitchen. "I'm making ribs in the crock pot, with potato salad."

I frowned. Definitely not my favorite. I was glad I didn't bring Scott. My mother made the worst potato salad, using Miracle Whip and dill. It was sweet and strange. Even the prison potato salad was better.

"Your father, of course, has to have beans."

"Of course," said Dom. "Where is he?"

"Tinkering in the garage. He found a weed-whacker on the side of the road and is trying to fix it."

"He knows how?"

"No idea."

"Maybe you should help him, Dom," said Evie.

"I wouldn't know the first thing about something like that."

Evie gave him a look that meant, "Do what I say." I waved at Dom as he skulked away to the garage.

Evie then said, "I'm going to the bathroom."

That left me alone with my mother. I knew what she was trying to do. It was a bad idea, I thought. I planned to tell them over dinner.

My mother cut up the cooked potatoes, dropping them into a large bowl. "So what's her name?"

"Whose name?"

"The girl you're seeing."

"I'm not seeing a girl."

"I thought you said you were busy."

"I am."

"That usually means you're dating someone."

"I am dating someone."

She paused for a minute as that sunk in. I don't know what I expected. Would she turn to me and yell at me, or would she hug me?

"Oh," was all she said, and kept on cutting up potatoes.

I thrust my hands in my pockets and tried to look innocent when Evie came back. She looked from me, to my mother, and back to me.

"Everything okay?" she asked.

"Fine," my mother said.

"Yeah," I said at the same time.

My mother didn't look at me when she got the dreaded Miracle Whip from the cabinet. She concentrated entirely on the construction of the potato salad.

"Need any help, mom?" I asked.

"No," she said. It wasn't anger, wasn't disappointed; it had no inflection whatsoever — at least none that I could tell.

"I'm going, um," I thumbed at the door to the garage. As I did, Dom walked in, my father following.

"It's dead, Jim," said Dom.

My father's hands were black with grease. He saw me, nodded, which was the best I was going to get. He was in a bad mood because he couldn't fix something. That happened more often than he wanted to admit.

My mother said, as he walked by her, "Mikey's here."

"I know," he said, and reached for the bottle of industrial cleaning goop he kept under the sink.

I swallowed. The scent of that soap mixing with the barbecue didn't work well. The thought of eating that potato salad almost, but not quite, turned my stomach.

Soon enough, mom had everything ready and we sat down to ribs falling off the bone and potato salad with dill weed. Dad and Dom had a beer, while Evie and I stuck with Coke, and my mom had lemon water.

We were settled down, in the middle of dinner. We were silent. My mother usually chattered up a storm, but she was quiet. Evie was quiet. My father tore chunks of meat off the bone and grunted as he ate. Dom kept his head down. And me … I wanted to come right out and tell them. But every time the words formed in my mind, my mouth wouldn't say them.

I kept looking at my father, barbecue slathered all over his face, and thinking, *What would Scott think of this Neanderthal?* What would Scott think of my parents: who wouldn't even understand what gay meant? My mother knew — at least I thought she knew — and that was most important to me.

"Tell them," said Grimalkin from behind my father. "Tell them the truth."

I stared at Grimalkin. He had never appeared so close to anyone before. He stood directly behind my father, his hands raised, as if to place them on my father's shoulders. Dom saw me staring at the air above my father, and he looked in the same direction.

"Mike?" he asked.

I broke away my gaze to focus on Dom. Dom was real. Grimalkin was not. I was losing it.

My parents didn't know about my condition, my sexual orientation, or my prison stay. We told them nothing. I was full of secrets from them. I set my rib down, wiped my face.

"I'm gay," I said suddenly.

My father stopped in mid-tear. "What?" he said with his mouth full.

"I'm gay," I said, a little louder.

Ribs fell on plates. Evie watched my father. Dom kept eating. My mother stared at her plate. And my father, who I expected to thunder and rant and haul off and throw something at me, glared at me with eyes so full of hate and disgust that I wanted to crawl under the table and be the worm he probably saw me as.

"I always knew you were worthless," he finally said.

"Dad!" Evie wiped her hands with the napkin. She moved to place her hand on my father's arm.

I turned away from him. I didn't know where to look. I focused on a ragged yellow-edged hole in the tablecloth next to my soda glass. That was unusual. My mother always had pristine linens.

Or did she not, and I never noticed it before?

"What are you going to do, wear dresses from now on?"

"No," I replied, now giving him a glare of my own.

"Makeup? Nail polish?"

"Dad, stop," said Evie. "It's not like that."

He snorted. "Don't bring your 'friend' around here."

"I wasn't planning on it."

My father pushed himself away from the table and got up. My mother watched him. "Is dinner okay?"

He threw a napkin on top of his half-eaten rib. "Too much sauce."

Without looking at me or Evie, he left the table and walked out to the living room. I heard the TV go on.

My mother got up and cleared his plate away, along with hers. Dom kept eating until Evie gave him an elbow in his side. I knew from experience that eventually my mother would sit without a plate in front of her and watch the rest of us eat, giving us a sorry smile which made us feel guilty: *If your father doesn't eat, neither do the rest of us.*

Evie picked up my plate before I could finish, and swiped Dom's plate as well. She joined my mother at the kitchen sink to wash dishes.

"Nice work, Mike," said Dom.

At least I didn't have to finish the potato salad.

We drove home in silence. My phone rang when we crossed the border into Rhode Island.

"Hello, Ritter."

"Grimaulkin. Appointment tomorrow at ten."

"I'll be ready."

"Are you in an airplane?"

"It's the car."

"You need a new one."

"We know."

"See you tomorrow."

He hung up first. "I have an appointment tomorrow," I said to Evie.

She just nodded. She hadn't said a word since we left.

It wasn't until after we got home when Evie opened the door and turned to me. "You didn't have to come right out and tell them."

Dom put the leash on Rufus and took him out. But I couldn't escape.

"How else was I supposed to tell them?"

"Let them down gently. I don't know!" She tore off her jacket and slammed it on the hook in the foyer. "Dad's probably yelling at Mom now, telling her it's all her fault."

"It's nobody's fault, Evie."

"They don't understand that."

"So what do you want me to do? Apologize? I won't apologize for what I am."

She dropped onto the stool in the kitchen. "What are we going to do with you, Mikey?"

"I'm going to try and get a job. Okay? Tomorrow. And then I'll move out and be out of your hair."

"It's not you, Mikey. It's … I don't know what to do anymore. Dom can't get anything permanent, I don't know how long I'll be subbing for, and you don't have anything, we need a new car, our rent is going up, and now our parents aren't going to talk to you anymore."

"The last is my problem. Do you want a permanent job there?"

"Everyone there is nice. The principal is nice. What I want to do is go back and become an administrator. There's no money in teaching."

"I'll get you a job. And Dom, too, if you want."

"I thought you can't do magic."

"Not magic," I said, trying to backpedal. "Maybe if I talk to my parole officer. He can put a word in. Or the library."

She shrugged. "I feel so helpless."

I put my arms around her and hugged her. "I'll help, I promise."

When Dom came back, Evie had already changed into sweats and was ready for bed. I fed Rufus while Dom got changed. Both of them retreated to the bedroom while I lay on the couch. Even I knew this was getting old.

The next morning I sat outside when Ritter's car pulled up. I got into the car. I felt something weird, something pressing down on me. I looked up at the roof of the car and noted the red fire of runes activated above my head.

"You okay?" he asked.

"Yeah," I said.

"That car you called me from, is it your sister's car?"

"Yeah. We don't have enough money to get it fixed."

Ritter checked traffic as he turned around in the parking lot. "We have a few older Lincolns that we could sell you."

"If we don't have the money to get it fixed, what makes you think we have the money to get another car?"

"I'll talk to some people."

Magic works, even on the people that use it.

If I thought I was pressured in the car, going into the Confessor's office was worse. There were runes everywhere. I tried to ignore them, but I kept getting distracted by the orange bursts out of the corner of my eye.

When the Confessor came out of his office to get me from the waiting room, he himself was covered in runic fire. That didn't happen before, even when I first saw him and first started taking the medicine.

He invited me in, and I walked in cautiously. It was like walking into purgatory. Fiery runes were all on the walls, their flames flowing into each other. The Confessor was a pillar of flame. However, when he sat down, his flames faded and I could see him clearly.

"When did you stop taking the Thorazine?"

"Huh?" I asked.

"You stopped taking the medicine."

"Yeah," I looked down.

"You can't go cold turkey on a medicine like that. It could bring back your psychosis in a much worse way." He sat back. "So when did you stop?"

"A couple of days ago."

"Can you see the sigils in the room?"

"Yes."

"Do you know what they are?"

"Not all of them. They're on fire."

"Ever seen that before?"

"Just my own magic sometimes."

"Do you see Grimalkin?"

"Not right now."

"When was the last time?"

"Yesterday."

"What did he say?"

I started tugging at the zipper of my jacket, moving it up and down. "He told me to tell my parents I'm gay."

"Did you?"

"Yes."

"How did that go over?"

I chuckled, "Not too well." I explained my parents' reactions.

"At least they didn't throw you out."

"I expected that. I didn't expect the silent treatment."

"It might take them a while to process it. In the meantime, what are you planning to do?"

"What do you mean?"

"You have magic again. What are your plans?"

"I want to help Dom get the job he wants. And Evie, too."

"So you're going to be casting spells. You know what's against your parole, right?"

"I'm not going to be summoning anything!"

"What do you plan on doing?"

"I don't know. Candle spells? River spells? Prayer?"

"You're not going to use Grimalkin for any of this, are you?"

"He might have knowledge I don't."

"It's your knowledge, just compartmentalized. You do know it, but part of you doesn't want you to."

"Why's that?"

"Did your Aunt Jane teach it to you?"

"Some stuff. The conjuring and some simple magic."

"The rest you learned in prison?"

"Yes. With Grimalkin."

He tilted his head. "How?"

"We practiced. I would learn and memorize whatever everyone told me, and we would practice back and forth."

"But you knew the magic wouldn't work in the prison."

"Some did."

The Confessor crossed his arms. The room's flames got higher, as if someone had turned up the gas on them. There was no heat, no further pressure on me.

"Like what?" he asked me.

"Like if there was a fight or if I wanted to hide. I could use the invisibility spell to make me not be seen."

"Can you do it now?"

"I don't need to. It works only if I need to. Isn't that part of magic?"

"True, that you need the will to do the magic, or, barring that, the need. What if you used it now to try and get past Ritter?"

"The sigils won't let me."

"But some of these are the same as in prison."

"Some, not all."

He bowed his head. "I'll grant you that. They might stop your spell from working. But the sigils in prison are far more powerful than my own."

"What are you saying? That all the magic I did in prison didn't happen?"

He didn't say anything, just looked at me with a small smile on his face.

"But people left me alone when I did invisibility spells."

"You don't have to use spells to be undetectable."

"What?"

"Ever hear of ninjas?"

"Yeah, of course."

"Ninjas claimed to use spells, but all they did was blend into their surroundings. You did the same thing."

"That's … that's not possible."

"Think about how many things that happen to you without spells."

I thought of Ritter offering the car. Of Scott saving me from Malachi putting my face through a car window.

The Confessor stood up. He wasn't on fire this time. "You have plenty to think about."

I got up as well. The fires had dimmed in the room.

He escorted me out, saying to Ritter, "Thursday, the usual time."

Ritter nodded once, and brought me out to the car. My mind was reeling. How could magic work on its own, without me to direct it?

When a tree falls in a forest and no one is around to hear it, does it make a sound?

"Are you going to the gym?" Ritter asked me.

"I didn't bring my gear."

I could teleport my gym clothes, but I preferred not to use that spell unless I had to. Who knew if the Rosicrucians would catch me using it. Though not quite a summoning, someone like Ritter could consider it to be one. I used the teleportation spell only if I had to.

"I can wait while you get it."

"No, I'll walk it."

He shrugged.

"It'll clear my head."

"Yeah. It usually does."

EIGHT

WORK

WHEN I GOT TO THE LIBRARY, I brought coffee to the girls, then went upstairs to check my mail, and saw that there was a sealed white business-sized envelope with *"Grimaulkin"* in calligraphy on it.

I looked around the room. Who the hell knew where my "mailbox" was? While standing at the pile of Congressional Records. I slit open the envelope along the length of its seam. After I pulled out a folded cream piece of paper, a business card fell out. It had the Rhode Island state seal on it and a name: Richard Jensen, Director of Detectives, State Police, with three phone numbers.

The note in the envelope said, "Call this man immediately and make an appointment to assist the police. Inform him you are from the Rosicrucians. You will be our liaison on the North Burial Ground case."

I sure as hell didn't ask for this. The note wasn't signed, but I knew it must have come from my parole officer.

I left the library, went across to the Y, and used the pay phone there. I had gone way over the minutes allowed on the cellular plan last month, so I tried to pay attention to my usage.

The first number was an answering machine. The second number said "Fax" next to it, which I assumed meant a cooler way of spelling "facts". Maybe it was a tip line? I dialed it and got an earful of a high-pitched shriek that sounded worse than the dial-up from AOL.

The third number said, "Cell", so I called that.

"Detective Jensen," said a deep baritone.

"Hello. I'm Mike LeBonte. I'm … um, the Rosicrucians sent me."

"You on a public phone?"

"Yes …"

"Where are you?"

"At the YMCA in downtown Pawtucket."

"Can you meet me at the Providence police station?"

"I don't have a car."

He paused for a minute. "How old are you?"

"Eighteen."

"Oh, great," I heard him mutter. "I'll send a car to get you." He hung up.

I put my things in a locker, spelled it so it couldn't be opened, and went back to the lobby. As I exited the building, I saw a gray state trooper car double-parked in front of the door.

"LeBonte?" yelled the trooper out the window at me.

"Yeah."

"Get in the back."

I got in, but realized there were no door handles on the inside. I had to use my nails to dig into the upholstery so I could shut the door. We drove with the sirens on.

It was fun, even as I was thrown from side to side in the back of the car because I didn't have a seat belt. We made it to the Providence police station in record time.

The police station was a behemoth of a building, *art deco* style — top of the line in the '40's, but rundown now. The trooper parked in the police yard, got out, and pulled open the door for me.

That's when I noticed he was a big guy, well-built and chiseled, deep Italian good looks. I think I stared at him a little too long.

"You okay?" he asked me.

"Yep! I'm just fine!"

I climbed out of the car. The pants he wore made him look perfect, as they were tight and stuffed into jackboots. He went first, so I had no choice but to watch his butt move under the tight brown material.

Not that that was a problem.

We went through the back of the station. Some of the Providence cops watched as the guy plowed his way through clutches of people gathered as if they weren't even there. I jogged at times to keep up with him.

He led me up two flights of stairs, past a bank of desks with people on phones or reading things, to a room in the back. All the blinds were drawn around the windows in this room. The trooper knocked on the door, opened it, and stepped aside to let me in.

There were five people in the room: three men and two women. They all stopped what they were doing when I stepped inside.

My eye was first caught by the wall: a large map of the state, with red pins stuck in different places. Red yarn led from the top to the middle, from the middle to the side.

Then I looked at the people. A light-skinned African-American man stood at the map. Next to him was a white guy in a suit, smaller than the first man I saw. One of the two women was seated, her hands hovering over the pictures strewn about the table. She wore a t-shirt and jeans. The other woman, wearing a business dress and heels, stood right next to me near the door. The last man was Reilly.

"You," said Reilly.

"Hi, again," I said with a smile to him.

The man near the map, in the baritone voice I had heard on the phone, said, "You know each other?" Obviously, this was Jensen.

"I called him first," said Reilly. "He said he couldn't help."

"The Rosy Cross sent him."

The woman seated at the table placed her hands down on the picture of the tombstone covered in blood. "It starts here."

"No kidding," said the other woman. She pursed her lips and crossed her arms.

"What do you know about Satanists?" Jensen asked me.

"There's different kinds," I said, repeating Grimalkin's voice in my mind. "There's the Anton LeVey kind, the theoretic kind, and the conjuring kind."

"This is a conjuration of many souls," said the seated woman.

I stared at her. She was a medium — not a good one, though. She was a good reader of the room, and would give them what they wanted to hear.

She stared back at me. I put up a psychic defense as I looked at her, a wall in my mind that I used to put up when faced with the Confessors in prison. She wasn't half as subtle as they were. She was taking a sledgehammer to my concrete wall. It would break through, but it was obvious, and going to cost her a lot of energy.

Show her who's boss, said Grimalkin.

I put both hands on the table and leaned in. "Melinda."

She gasped, the sledgehammer falling away, and she put a hand to her chest, gripping something through her shirt.

"Why don't you let the big boys handle this?"

She pushed back away from me, scrambled to get away, making the sign of the cross as she bolted out the door.

"Well," said Reilly. "The magician wins over the gypsy."

"Could have told you she was a waste of time," said the other woman.

"Anyway," said Jensen to me. "You saw the scene at the North Burial Ground. There have been two other scenes like it since."

"Did that kid at Blackstone Boulevard have anything to do with this?"

"We think so."

"You said they summoned Lucifer," said Reilly.

"Yes," I said.

"Can they do it over a period of time?"

"They?" *Oh, my God,* I thought. *A cult.*

"There's more than one scene," said the man near the map, "so there must be more than one person."

"There are slight differences," added the woman.

I walked over to the map. One pin was in Woonsocket. The other pin was in Foster. One in Cranston; another in Providence.

"Are you trying to see a pattern?"

"Yes," said the man whose name I didn't know.

"It's not that."

"What is it, then?"

"What kind of blood was on the tombstones?"

"Human blood," said the woman. "A mixture of people. No one type."

"So it *is* a cult. The state is small enough to go to different places in an hour or less."

"But would they summon Lucifer at all these places?"

"Not necessarily," I said. "They may be sacrificing to him, feeding him. One person may have allowed himself to be possessed. Or … or even a few people. They would have to offer up their blood to keep Lucifer with them." *Maybe.* Grimalkin was telling me all this, and I wasn't believing it myself. *Could that be true?*

"Then again," I said, as Grimalkin told me what to say next, and my stomach dropped to the floor, "Lucifer may be a free spirit, available to do their bidding."

Jensen stood back. The man whose name I didn't know was the only one who said, "Shit."

"What about Malachi?" I asked Reilly.

He shook his head. "He just came to Pawtucket last week. He lives in a one-room apartment in Central Falls."

Damn, he wouldn't be involved.

The woman said, "So now what?"

"Wait for the bodies to pile up."

"That's impossible," said Reilly.

I stared at the map, listening to Grimalkin's voice in my head. I didn't want to utter what he was saying: *Tell them you could summon Lucifer from them if he's a free spirit.* But then he'd possess me, and I knew that. Gaining control of Lucifer was a magician's dream. But Lucifer was a crafty demon, and he didn't surrender easily. He had to be placated, tempted, flattered — then bound.

The detectives talked among themselves. I wasn't listening because Grimalkin was getting more and more insistent. I closed my eyes, to try and focus, but that didn't help. Someone called my name: the man I didn't know.

"Can you sense the spirit if it's free?"

I licked my lips. "Yes and no. I can summon him to me, but I can't see where he came from, and I can't see where he belongs. And most of all, I can't bind him, so he can hurt me and anyone around me if I don't have the right protective measures in place."

"What do you need?"

"Most places, even Salem, wouldn't have what I need. Got any virgin black goats with a white spot on her head hanging around?"

Reilly burst out laughing. The other three didn't look quite as amused.

"I've never done the actual ritual," I said. "It's all theory as far as I know." *Theory and the word of a demon in my head.* "I don't think the Rosicrucians would let me do it, even if I could get all the materials."

"We need to catch them before they act," said Jensen. "Any ideas?"

I closed my eyes, held my finger out, and walked up to the map until my finger hit it. I opened my eyes to see where I was pointing.

Newport.

A different, but still cute, state trooper took me back to the apartment. I felt both like a prisoner and a high-ranking politician, being driven around in the back of a cruiser, although this time without the lights and sirens.

"Thank you, sir," I said to him when he opened the back door for me to get out.

"You're welcome," he said.

It was just before dinner. The car wasn't in the driveway. Maybe they were running late.

I went upstairs, opened the door to see Evie in the kitchen and Dom on the couch, watching TV. Rufus came up to me as usual.

"Hey," I said, giving Evie a quick kiss on the cheek. "What happened to the car?"

"What do you mean 'What happened to the car?'" asked Evie.

"It's not outside in the driveway."

"Dom? Did you park on the street?"

"No," he said, turning the TV down. "What's the matter?"

"I didn't see the car," I said.

"You didn't see …" Dom, in a pair of shorts and barefoot, came around the couch and headed out the door, Rufus following without his leash.

I snapped up the leash as Evie called after the dog, and I dashed after everyone.

"Oh, shit!"

Dom thrust his hands in his short hair as he stood out in the November air, staring at the spot the green Camry had been.

I caught Rufus and hooked the leash on him as Evie said, "Who would have stolen it?"

"Kids. Damn kids. Dammit!" Dom stomped on the stubble of lawn.

I turned to look at the street and saw a dark blue Lincoln four-door sedan sitting there. It looked in perfect condition, if a little big, and too fancy for this neighborhood.

"Mike?" Evie called. She held a 9-x-12 white rectangular envelope in her hand. "This is addressed to you."

I took the envelope, saw *Grimaulkin* scrawled in old-fashioned cursive. Nobody knew my address. I opened the clasp and peered inside.

A set of black keys sat at the bottom of the envelope. I fished them out and stared at them.

A piece of yellow and blue paper followed them. It looked like it had been printed out on an old-fashioned printer with holes on the side of the paper. It said, "State of Rhode Island Vehicle Registration". On it was Dom's name and address. I handed it to Evie.

Last inside the envelope was a piece of what seemed like vellum — a colorful red, white, and blue paper with seals and signatures, saying at the top, "Title".

Evie walked over to the blue car in front of the house. She looked at the license plate on the back. Dom watched Evie.

"Dom," she called to him. I walked over to them as they gathered at the back of the car.

The registration number on the yellow paper matched the license plate.

"What the hell?" Dom took the registration from Evie and studied it.

I grinned and handed him the keys. "Take her out for a spin."

"Let me see that." He took the Title out of my hand and turned it over. "It belonged to a company fleet, so it doesn't have a name on it."

Evie said to me, "Mike, do you know something about this?"

"They mentioned you should get a new car." I touched the trunk. "I didn't expect this."

"They?"

"The Rosicrucians."

Dom, still barefoot, picked his way around the car. "It's been inspected and registered for two years. It's a 1997 — only three years old."

"Go get your shoes on and take it out."

He gave the keys to Evie, then dashed upstairs.

"Did you ask for this?" Evie asked, her hand on her hip.

"I didn't ask. They offered."

"What do you have to do in exchange?"

"Work for them, I guess."

She tilted her head, and pursed her lips.

"It's okay. The work isn't too hard and the pay's pretty good."

Evie smiled. She unlocked the car and peered inside. "Leather seats! Oh, my God, power windows! Is that air conditioning?"

I looked in the back. "You could have a party in the back seat."

Dom returned wearing shoes, pants, a shirt and hooded sweatshirt. "C'mon, Evie."

"I'll wait here," I said. I'd ridden in Ritter's Lincoln. I knew how they handled. They wouldn't be back for hours.

The next afternoon, Scott took out the tarot cards and laid them out in a fan shape on the counter in the store. Sometimes he felt the need to tell fortunes.

"Pick a card, Mike."

I picked a card and handed it to him. He laid it above the fan. It pictured a single stick with crystals at both ends, and a pair of sunflowers at its base. The stick had lines around it, as if it were a shining sun.

"Power," he said. "The beginning of an enterprise."

My magic was back. I said, "Are you going to say: 'With great power comes great responsibility?'"

"You already know that."

I looked out the window. "I think I know what that means." I got up. "Want anything from the restaurant?"

"Sure. Can you order us lunch?"

"You want your usual?"

Scott smiled, put the cards together. "Sure." He took out a ten-dollar bill from the till and gave it to me.

I walked down the hill to the restaurant. The "Now Hiring" sign was still up.

I stepped inside. It was before the lunch rush, so the place wasn't very busy. I plucked the sign from the window and laid it on the counter.

The waitress came over to me, saw me with my hand on the sign. "I can start tomorrow, but I have an appointment on Thursday at ten, so I have to leave early."

The waitress looked over at the grill cook. The grill cook was a heavy-set man, short, his face red and puffy. The blue Red Sox cap on his head hid most of his very short black hair. He seemed not to be paying attention, but he said, "Works for me." He flipped a burger, laid it on some bread, and set it on a plate. He came over to me. "What's your name?"

"Mike."

"Chris."

"Good to meet you." I shook his hand.

"Likewise. Ever work in a kitchen before?"

"No."

"Good. No bad habits. Come in tomorrow at five."

"I'll be here." I turned to the waitress. "Oh, I'd like a turkey sandwich with bacon and mayo, and a cheeseburger with large fries."

"I'm Donna."

I smiled at her. "Hi."

She only nodded as she took down my order.

I sat at the counter. "So what will I be doing when I come in?"

Chris kept working on stuff on the grill. "Cleaning up, busing, chopping, doing some of the simple stuff for the breakfast rush. Prepping for lunch. I'd rather have you out of the way for the lunch rush."

"Which is why it's five to eleven."

"Saturdays, too. You can take Tuesday and Sunday off. It's not that busy on Tuesdays."

"I can do that."

"Saturday, we do breakfast all day. You might work extra hours on that day if it's busy."

It would give Evie time to clean, or Dom and Evie to spend time alone. After work, I could go to the library and the gym, or to Scott's for a little while.

"I'll pay you on Saturday. Is that okay, or do you need it on Friday?"

"Saturday is fine. The rent isn't due until Sunday."

"No time clocks."

"How do you know the hours I'll work?"

"I'll know."

Donna handed me a bag. Chris made the cheeseburger so fast I didn't even notice. "He does know, too."

I picked up the bag. "Thanks. I'll see you bright and early tomorrow."

"Later, Mike."

When I walked out, I knew I had accomplished something.

NINE

FIRST DAY

I THOUGHT DOM WAS GOING TO BREAK OUT CHAMPAGNE when I told him that I was starting a job tomorrow. Evie hugged me and made mac and cheese out of a box with hot dogs for our dinner. Not Dom's favorite, but it was mine.

We sat down on the couch and watched some sitcom where I didn't get half the jokes. Evie and Dom were happy.

They dug out an old alarm clock and set it up in the living room, setting it for 3:45 a.m. This gave me enough time for me to get up, stumble to the shower, and get ready for work. I'd have an hour to walk to work, even though I walked fast, and could get there much earlier.

I didn't pack my gym stuff, because I didn't know how tired I'd be after work. I did bring my finished library books in my gym bag.

At 3:45 Wednesday morning, the damn thing buzzed loud enough to wake the dead. I reached over and shut it off, my ears ringing. I got up and went to the bathroom, took a shower, and came out with just a towel.

"Now I know why I put that alarm clock in the closet," said Evie, standing in the doorway to their bedroom. She saw me and turned around.

I laughed, dropped the towel, and got dressed.

"You're not going to be up every morning, are you?"

"No. I wanted to see you off on your first day." She still faced the bedroom as she spoke.

I finished getting dressed, then tapped her shoulder. I wore jeans and a red t-shirt. "What do you think?"

"You look good," she said.

I hugged her, put on my sneakers, grabbed my coat, my bag, and my wallet.

"Go back to bed," I told her. "You've got two hours."

She waved her hand, yawned, and went back to the bedroom. I pet Rufus, who looked confused.

"I'll take you out when I get back, okay? New routine."

I walked in the dark to the restaurant. As I expected, I got there at 4:28 a.m. There was one car in the parking lot in the back: a square-shaped brown car with rust spots all over the back driver-side wheel. I saw light peering out of the back door of the restaurant. I knocked on it.

Chris opened the door for me. "You're early."

"I didn't know how long it would take me to walk here."

"You have to walk?" He stepped aside to let me in.

"It's no big deal. Takes me about twenty minutes. Thirty, if I walk slow."

"Coffee's brewing," he said, as he walked through the cramped back room.

Boxes were stacked neatly against the wall. Against the wall that separated the patrons from the kitchen, was a clean, white counter with a double metal sink next to it. Against the wall behind that, facing the back of the kitchen, sat a large almost-white gas stove. Pots and pans hung from the ceiling; ladles and large spoons hung from hooks in the ceiling as well.

"I don't drink coffee," I said, sniffing the dark roast-infused air.

"You from Mars or something?" Chris asked with a smile. "Everybody drinks coffee around here."

"Connecticut. I drink tea."

He shook his head. "Tea bags are next to the coffee machine. You get the water from the machine. The red button over there, see?"

He pointed to a red spigot sticking out of the coffee machine. I got a mug and put two tea bags in it, then poured the scalding hot water into the mug.

"Ever handle a knife before?"

"Just a little."

"Know how to pare potatoes?"

"You peel them?"

He laughed. "Yeah, and cut them up into chunks, about an inch square."

He brought me over to a bag and bent to lift it.

"I got it," I said, and easily lifted the fifty-pound bag of potatoes. "Where do you want them?"

"On the table next to the counter."

I set them down there. He slit open the bag, got a paring knife and deftly peeled a potato, then cut it up into the chunks the size he wanted.

"Don't worry if there's some skin or black spots. Except if it's really big in the middle. Cut those out." He pointed to a black apron on a hook. "Use that so you don't get too dirty."

"Okay."

He put a large stock pan in the sink, poured water into it about half way. "Put the potatoes in here as you go along."

I went to work. It was actually difficult. I was used to using a potato peeler, not a knife to peel potatoes, so I ended up cutting too much potato off. He came back after a little while to see my pitiful pile of potatoes in the pan.

"You gotta go faster, Mike, or you'll be here all morning." He put his hand in the water and lifted some potatoes out. "They don't have to be perfectly one-inch square. They're gonna be home fries tomorrow and mashed potatoes for later."

"Sorry," I muttered.

He smiled. "You're new, I get it. You just gotta practice more. Practice is the heart of learning."

"Thanks."

"Don't mention it. I want that bag done by the time I finish making the meatloaf."

I moved faster, though I did cut myself and too much potato. But I wasn't as particular about the chunks this time.

I had three potatoes to go when he returned to the back room with a metal tray of three raw meatloaves on it. "Almost done!" I said.

"Good," he said. "When you're done that, rinse off the potatoes. Divide them into two pans and put them on the stove to boil. With water."

"Got it."

After the potatoes came washing down the tables, booths and stools, washing the six pans I had used to try and judge how much was half of the stockpot full of potatoes I had to peel, and chopping onions. He let me sit down and cry after I did that, as he leaned against the counter, drinking his third mug of coffee and waiting for the grill to heat up.

"If someone says, 'Hot pan', don't move, okay? That means someone's walking behind you with a hot pan or something that could break."

The back door squealed open.

"This is Wendy," he said, as a young woman, blond with brown roots, and deep blue eyes stepped in.

She was shorter than me, had a round and happy face — unlike Donna, who was older, wrinkled, and looked ready to spit nails.

"Hey, honey," she said, her Southern accent very apparent in those two words. "You got someone!" She came up to me. "Hey, sugar, I'm Wendy."

"Mike," I said, taking her hand.

"Pleasure is all mine," she said. "Chris's been a real bear since Al left. The last guy was a real piece." She rolled her eyes.

Chris shrugged. "Have your coffee and then open up, would you?"

"Sure, sugar," she said, and winked at me.

She pulled on an apron and got a mug of coffee.

"What do I do?" I asked.

"Stay in the back, come out when I call you or when you're done with the dishes, and bus the tables. Take the tips and put them in the jar over here," he showed me a Mason jar under the cash register. "We do the rush from when we open until about nine."

"I have to leave then, tomorrow," I said. I'd have to walk to the house and wait for Ritter.

"Oh, yeah, right. You got an appointment. Tomorrow's special is chili. Real easy to put together. I'll show you."

Wendy drank her coffee fast, opened the door. She handed the empty mug to me.

"First dish you get to wash today, honey."

I trudged back home, not even bothering to hit the library drop — off box. I was on my feet for almost the entire time, busing tables, washing dishes. I understood why it was called a "rush" — as soon as one person would leave, there was another person waiting for the spot.

There were regulars, who called me "the new kid". I didn't stick around up front because I had to make sure there were clean dishes for Chris to use. I had to be fast, and I had to be clean, because if anyone found a speck of something from someone else's breakfast on their dish, they'd freak out. I knew that I would.

Wendy came and helped me for the first hour or so, drying and stacking dishes for Chris out front. There were piles of clean dishes in the back, but we weren't supposed to use them.

"Those are for the weekend," Wendy told me.

It was faster and easier to use a set amount of dishes during the week when it wasn't as busy.

A pile of dishes remained for me to do by the time I left. There was no way I was going to get them done by eleven. I looked around, placed them all in the water, and twirled my finger around in the water, muttering a spell to clean them. I took them out, one at a time, and dried them off, inspecting each one.

Yep, the spell worked. I had a feeling I was going to be using that spell a lot.

As soon as I opened the door to the apartment, Rufus came at me, expecting to go out.

"Oh, God, Rufus, not now."

I wanted to collapse on the couch and catch a nap. Dom came out of the bathroom, naked.

He and I looked at each other. He blushed and ducked back into the bathroom to retrieve a towel.

"It's nothing I haven't seen before, Dom," I called after him.

"Ha, ha." He came back out with a towel around his waist. "Listen, I have an interview to go to."

"That's good. For where?"

"A new paper called *The Valley Breeze*."

"Do you need a good luck amulet?"

He hesitated at the door to the bedroom. "I suppose it couldn't hurt."

I stole a piece of paper out of the printer and sat at the computer desk. I used a normal ball-point pen to draw the sigil on the paper, and then folded it into a triangle. When Dom came out in his suit, I tucked it in his breast pocket.

"Thanks, Mike."

"Don't mention it. Good luck."

He took the keys and waved goodbye. I plopped down on the couch. Rufus realized he wasn't going out, so he lay down next to me. I closed my eyes, intending to doze off.

It seemed like only minutes later that the phone rang. I picked it up off the cradle.

"Hey, Mike," said Scott, cheerfully. "How was your first day?"

"Exhausting."

I lay back on the couch, holding the phone close to my ear. Rufus lay across my feet. I glanced at the clock on the cable box. I had fallen asleep for two hours.

"I had to peel potatoes and wash dishes."

"That's no fun."

"That's why it's called work, right?"

We talked about how the people were, details of what I had to do. He then asked me, "Want to come over for dinner? I promise I won't make you wash dishes."

I sat up. "Will you bring me to work in the morning?"

"I suppose I could do that," he said.

I could hear the smile in his voice.

⊗　　⊗　　⊗

Dinner consisted of stuffed shells, linguini, and Scott for dessert. Four-thirty in the morning, we stumbled out of his apartment. Scott was still in his slippers as he drove me to the restaurant.

"Imagine walking in the snow to work, Mike."

"I can imagine that."

Scott pulled his car around back, gave me a kiss, and yawned in my face. I chuckled, patted him on the cheek. He acted as tired as I felt.

Chris was already peeling potatoes when I walked in. "Morning," I said.

"Hey," he said. "Thought I'd get these started."

"Sorry I'm slow."

"You'll pick up speed. Since I only have you 'til nine, I want you to go clean up front. Get the vacuum and broom and go sweep up. Okay?"

"Okay."

Chris seemed to read my body. If I had to stand there and peel potatoes, I would have fallen asleep. It was a good thing I did a lot of moving around. It helped me to wake up. I lifted the rugs and swept, vacuumed, and washed the floors. I washed the counters, booths and stools. I even washed the cash register, using a screwdriver to get in between the keys.

Donna arrived, grunted at me, grabbed a cup of coffee, and opened up — all without being told to. I retreated to the back room and stayed out of Donna's way. It wasn't that she scared me; I just didn't want to make her mad at me.

When I finished the dishes around 8:30, the place had two people in it. Chris leaned against the counter, talking to the man I called "The Preacher", because he asked me a few times if I believed in God. I hustled away before I could answer him.

But this time, there was no escape as I stood in the doorway waiting for someone to finish so I could bus the table.

"Do you believe in God?" asked the Preacher of me.

"Yes," I said.

"And his only begotten son?"

"No."

Chris laughed. "So you're Jewish?"

"No," I said. "I'm … reformed."

"How's that?"

I looked from Chris to The Preacher, back to Chris. I didn't want to lose my job on the second day.

"It's complicated."

"Try me," said Chris, his arms crossed.

"Okay," I said, and looked Chris in the eye. "I'm a magician."

"You pull rabbits out of hats?"

"No."

"A sorcerer," The Preacher muttered, getting his Bible, and holding it close to his chest. He fumbled in his pocket for money, threw down some dollar bills. He stood up, shaking his finger at me. "Blasphemy! Demon spawn!"

He hobbled out.

Chris raised an eyebrow. "Guess we're not going to be seeing him anymore." He cleared the dishes himself. "Good riddance, if you ask me."

"You don't believe in God?" I asked Chris.

"Let's just say I don't live my life by a book or what a guy who wants my money tells me to believe."

I liked this guy more and more.

He glanced at the clock. "You can go, if you need to. It's only fifteen minutes."

"Okay, thanks."

"You were here early yesterday. Don't mention it."

I took off my apron, hung it up next to the sink, and left by the back door.

Ritter was already parked in front of my house as I turned the corner. He saw me, because he pulled out of the spot and met me at the Modern Diner parking lot.

"Where were you?" he asked me.

I sighed as I finally sat down. "Working."

"Where?"

"Downtown. The Coffee Cup restaurant."

"When did you start there?"

"Yesterday." I stretched out my legs. "God, my feet hurt."

"Do you wait tables?"

"Busboy."

Although he didn't say it was good that I finally got a job, the Confessor did. The Confessor wasn't on fire today. I wondered why, but didn't ask him.

"A job will help you with your identity. It will give you something to do, and ways to interact with people." He motioned to the room. "Speaking of identity, have you seen Grimalkin lately?"

I didn't want to go into the whole thing with the police. "No."

The Confessor nodded. "That sounds promising. However, with your new job, do you want to come in the afternoons?"

"I get off at eleven. Except on Saturdays."

"How does twelve on Monday sound?"

"Sure. I hope I get used to it."

The Confessor smiled. "You will."

I had Ritter drop me off at the library, where I deposited my books. I happened to go look in the magazine room, which was on the way to the New Fiction area.

Malachi sat under the window, reading *Esquire.*

I froze. This library was *my* domain. How dare he come and plant himself here! I felt all my muscles bunch up, getting ready for a fight.

He calmly turned the page.

He doesn't know you're here, said Grimalkin. *This isn't the place for a fight.*

"I should avoid him?" I whispered. As I spoke the words, my body seemed to relax.

For now.

I ducked between the rear stacks to avoid his line of sight. I used the pent-up energy to duck and weave until I got to the Fiction section. A metal desk and chair faced the wall, usually used for people who wanted to have quiet time.

I straddled the chair and looked out down the aisle, to see the edge of the magazine rack. Grimalkin stood next to me.

"Is he hunting me?" I asked him.

"You're being paranoid," Grimalkin replied. "This isn't prison. He doesn't live his life to hurt you."

A little voice in my head said that was wrong, but it was just a peep — a nagging feeling more than a voice. I trusted

Grimalkin with my life thus far, and he hadn't been wrong yet. I stood up from the chair, and turned away from him, to the fiction shelves.

"I think I'll go with a classic," I said out loud, but Grimalkin was gone. I picked out *The Scarlet Letter.*

When I came out of the stacks, Malachi was gone, too. However, *Esquire* was on the floor next to the chair.

Disgusted because he was trashing *my* place, I picked it up and put it back. Lilly, the librarian at the desk, saw me and nodded as I put it in its alphabetically correct place. I went to the desk to check out my book.

I left the library to see Malachi standing at the corner, smoking a cigarette. I could throw the book at him and brain him.

He turned around to see me, then sauntered toward me. "Hey," he said. "No hard feelings, right?"

"You stay away from my boyfriend," I said, my body tensing up again.

"I don't swing that way, Grim."

"Well, *Mal,*" I said, "I want to make it perfectly clear that he's off limits to you at all times."

He chuckled. "You don't own him. This isn't Little Willie's bosom."

That's what some of the long-in-the-tooth prisoners called William F. Blackstone Prison. I never knew why, and no one told me. I was too busy learning spells.

"He's under my protection," I said. "I don't own him, but he's under me."

"I'm sure," Malachi said, leering at me.

I poked him in the chest. "Go near him, and I swear by the Five Rivers of Hell I'll send you there myself."

"Tough words, wizard." He backed up a step. "I believe you could do just that."

I blinked. *What?*

"He's all yours."

With that, he walked past me, up the hill, past the Y and the library, and kept on walking up the street until all I saw was a speck of black in the distance.

"You won," said Grimalkin as he leaned against a "No Parking" sign.

Did I?

TEN

THE CULT

T HE STATE TROOPER CAME INTO THE COFFEE CUP RESTAURANT and said, "I'm looking for Mike."

It was Saturday afternoon around two, and we were in the process of trying to chase out the remaining customers so we could close up. I stood next to a booth, holding the bucket that contained the dirty dishes.

"I'm Mike."

"They want you in the city."

I glanced at Chris.

"Go," he said, with a wave of his hand.

I finished clearing the dishes, tossed them in the sink, hung up my apron and followed the trooper out to the car. This time I rode in the front seat. This trooper had Hispanic features, with darker skin than mine, and short black hair under his gray Smokey-the-Bear hat.

"What's going on?" I asked.

"Some guy says he's possessed."

"I'm not a priest."

He shrugged as he sped down the highway. "You did this kind of thing in Pawtucket, right?"

Was I that famous?

"Yeah, but the dog died." And I inherited Belial for a time.

"Let's hope you got better at it."

I had no tools — not even a wand. I had no idea how I was supposed to perform a banishment without tools.

We ended up at Rhode Island Hospital. The state trooper guided me to a locked unit, where I saw people in varying degrees of insane distress. There was a guard outside of one room, watching the person inside.

The person was tied down to the bed, spread-eagle. A blanket covered him up to the middle of his chest. He was pale, skinny, probably in his early 20's, with short, sweat-soaked hair. He gazed at the ceiling and tugged at the restraints a couple of times, testing them.

The cop outside the room nodded to me. "He's been quiet."

"I'll come in with you," said the trooper, as he opened the glass door and allowed me to step inside.

I felt naked. I had no tools. Nothing but another cop with a gun, and this guy was supposed to be possessed. I wanted a crowd of people in case something happened.

The man turned his head when I entered. "Hey, man," he said.

"Hey," I said. "So tell me what's going on."

"Let me out of these things and I'll tell you."

"I can't do that."

He gazed at the ceiling again. He sighed heavily. "I won't do anything."

"Nope, sorry."

"Then I'm not going to tell you anything."

"Who possesses you?"

He laughed suddenly. "It's not a possession. It's an equal partnership."

"I hate to tell you, but demons don't work that way."

"How do you know?"

"I've summoned demons before."

I didn't look at the cop. I didn't know what he would think.

"Not this demon. He's the first fallen angel. He's naturally good and powerful."

Lucifer.

The door opened and two other people came in: one was a burly man, the other was a female nurse in scrubs.

"Who are you?" she asked me.

"Jensen asked for him," said the trooper.

"Jensen's not here. We're not going to play into this man's psychosis."

"I know something you don't know," the man sing-songed. "I know about the Iron Cult and you don't."

"What about them?" I asked. I never heard of that.

"I won't tell, I won't tell, I won't tell …"

"I can make you tell."

He turned his head and laughed at me.

Oh, that pissed me off.

"Get me a marker," I said. "A pen, something."

"I'm sorry," said the nurse. "But you need to leave."

I saw a pen in her pocket on her sleeve and plucked it out.

"Hey!"

I bent down on the floor and tried to scribble a coercion symbol on the linoleum. The pen didn't register the lines, but I forced my will into it. Dots appeared on the linoleum, but my magic made the lines connecting them.

The man tugged again at the restraints. "You can't, you can't—!"

Then the man on the bed started convulsing, yanking hard against the restraints. The nurse and the orderly ran out of the room, presumably to get the doctor.

I stood up and beckoned at the trooper. "Stand at the door."

He did, and I joined him, drawing a protective circle around us both in front of the door.

The man in the bed stopped convulsing. He lay still now, breathing heavily.

"What is the Iron Cult?" I demanded from my spot near the door.

"Something you wish you could join, Michael."

The voice was still the man's, but the man didn't speak the words. He slowly sat up — the restraints had somehow come undone, the straps unbuckled.

The trooper moved behind me. I glanced back to see he had drawn his weapon.

"That's not going to help," I said.

The man in the bed grinned at me. The blanket had fallen away. He was naked and didn't seem to care.

"Let him shoot me, set me free from this body to join my brethren."

He swung off the bed, placed his feet on the floor. He bent over to see the sigil I had drawn on the floor.

"Very good work, Michael. You learned well. But not well enough."

He moved fast, coming at us. I trusted my protective circle, and it did what it was supposed to: held him back. I saw the circle buckle when he hit it. The electricity shocked him and threw him back against the bed, shoving it sideways into the machines behind it.

"I stand corrected," the man said.

"Let me by," ordered a man behind me.

The guard outside held him back.

The naked man paced the room, looking at me and my circle to try and find a weakness. I searched my mind for the banishment ritual for Lucifer, but nothing came to me. I mean … it wasn't like I summoned Lucifer all the time.

"Grimalkin," I called.

The man grinned. "He's not real. Too bad for you."

He walked up to the circle and placed his hand in the air, pressing against the protective shield. He pushed against it, gritting his teeth against the pain. I smelled burning flesh as he kept trying to push into the field, inches away from my face. If I moved, he could possibly get closer. If I stayed still, he wouldn't get past me.

Then, the trooper shoved me forward and broke the circle. I fell forward, into the man's arms.

He embraced me, pressing his body against mine. "We need to stop meeting like this, Michael," he said, and held me tight, like a lover.

I tried to push away, but he was strong. I stomped hard on his foot in an attempt to distract him with pain. He didn't let go. I wouldn't look into his eyes, because I knew — I just knew — that he would possess me in that instant.

"Let go," he purred.

Then the trooper and an orderly pulled him off me. I backed away, keeping my eyes on his chest, not his face or eyes.

The man let them pull him back for a moment. The doctor pushed past me with the nurse as the trooper and the orderly manhandled the man back to the bed. The man gave them a token struggle.

He pulled an arm out of the orderly's grip and punched the trooper right in the face. The trooper let him go and he came after me.

"By the holy name of God, Yahweh," I yelled, the words suddenly coming to me, "I banish thee. I banish thee, Lucifer. I banish thee."

That made him pause, just long enough for the doctor to shoot him up with a tranquilizer.

He turned to the doctor and shoved him against the wall, but the doctor had gotten him with the sedative. The man slowly turned to face me. His eyes started to close. He took two steps toward me and buckled to his knees. Then he fell face-first at my feet.

Two other orderlies came in and lifted him back onto the bed.

The trooper holstered his gun. "I think you need a priest."

I nodded. This was magic that was beyond me — especially because I didn't know the right ritual and had no tools. They buckled him in, though I knew that wouldn't hold him again.

"If you get a priest," I said, "even if he isn't possessed, he thinks he is."

The doctor glared at me. "We got this," he said in a condescending tone.

"He's still under arrest," said the trooper.

"What for?" I asked.

"Murder," said the trooper.

Another soul fed into the existence of Lucifer, I thought. *How many more people would die before we took him down?*

I started adding things up as we left the room. This was another killing by Lucifer. Lucifer didn't seem to inhabit one body, but many at a time. I assumed he could do that, though my knowledge of that demon was sketchy. If that was the case, then there was a Satanic cult involved.

How many people were in the cult? Who was involved? Were they from all over the state?

"Where did this killing happen?"

"Warwick," said the trooper. "We caught him on the highway trying to escape."

"Have you already gone through his stuff?"

The trooper turned to me. "What do you mean?"

"Like who he knows; who he's interacted with. Notes, papers … that kind of thing."

"I'll call my supervisor and ask."

He stopped by a nurse's desk in the ER that was on the way out and called.

He held his hand over the speaker. "They're at the subject's house right now. What do you want them to look for?"

"Papers, diaries …"

"We do that anyway. We have his computer."

I had forgotten about the computer. I knew that AOL had a Satanic chat room, but I avoided it.

"That, too."

"We'll meet them in Lincoln."

We went back out to the car.

"What's your name, by the way?" I asked him.

"Sergeant Danny Costa."

"Thanks for doing this."

He smiled. "You owe me coffee."

"I don't have any money."

I realized that today was payday, but I had left without getting my money.

"How about where you work?"

"Oh, there! I'll give you breakfast myself."

"Deal," he said, and let me in the car.

They had already logged into the computer. Five men in suits gathered around a man seated at a keyboard and monitor. I stepped back, not wanting to crowd the man any more than he already was.

He finally got into the computer, and everyone peered at the monitor. I itched to get closer.

"Look at his bookmarks," someone said.

"What's NE Fallen?" asked another man.

"Angelfire website," said the man at the desk. "It's a free website for —"

"Demon summoners?"

I slapped my forehead.

Of course.

"New England fallen angels," I said from the back of the room. "Probably demon summoners in the New England area."

"Satanic cults?" asked someone, still looking at the screen, but not at me.

"That too. It's not the same," I said.

"There's a contact person here." Everyone took out pens and paper, taking down the contact name.

Another man spoke up. "What about his own website? You can do one on some free sites like Angelfire."

They discussed things like coding, and all sorts of acronyms I didn't know. I wanted to see the NE Fallen website, so I made a mental note to go check it out when I got home.

They signed onto his AOL account, as he had left his password written down on a sticky note on the computer. They printed out all his emails that had arrived recently and the ones he had saved. I didn't get to see them.

I was crowding the room, so I left it.

I found Danny in a common area, drinking coffee. He saluted me with the paper cup.

"Any luck?"

"There's a lot of people in there. I figured I'd wait until it wasn't so crowded."

Danny sipped his coffee. "Everything's going to be on computers, soon."

"Not me. Give me paper and pen anytime."

"Old school. You'll be behind the times, old man."

I laughed. I was probably ten years younger than Danny. "Do you have tea over there?"

"No, just coffee."

I shuddered. "I'll drink water."

"There's filtered water from the faucet."

I poured myself a paper cup of water and watched the door to see if anyone from the computer room was going to come out.

"You know," I said to Danny. "You seem to be taking this pretty good."

"Taking what?"

"Demons and magic and all that. I thought you would have shot the guy in the room when he came after us."

"Well," he said, leaning back. "My mother is a *bruja* — a witch."

"No kidding?"

He shrugged. "This weirdness is familiar. But my mother never did anything with demons."

"Just spirits?"

"Sometimes. Spells. Love and revenge spells, mostly."

"Do you know any?"

He waved his hand from side to side. "Bits and pieces. She never taught me. It's what I could get from watching her and my sisters."

I drank the water. Too bad he didn't know any spells. I would love to learn more of that kind of magic.

"I'm going to take a walk back to the computer room."

"I'll come with you."

He followed me down the hall. When I peeked into the room. No one was inside.

I walked in, and saw that the computer was still on, connected to AOL. "You've got mail," it chirped.

I glanced at Danny.

"I see nothing," he said.

I nearly jumped into the chair in front of the computer and opened the mail. It was addressed to Mackilroy23 and came from Ashmodai. Ashmodai was another name of Asmodeus, a demon controlling lust from the *Lesser Key of Solomon.*

RE: Meeting

We are now Five. HE is unsatisfied with your sacrifice at the Bright Moon. You must Sacrifice at the Dark Moon or HE will Withdraw HIS Graces. We will assist HIM in HIS wishes.

Hail Lucifer!

Ashmodai

"Five of them," said Danny. "Five Satanists."

I scanned through the email to see who sent him notes.

"There's two other demon names: Valafar and Dantalion."

"Then we have to go through each one of the emails to find out if they're from Satanists."

"Hey, what're you doing here?"

We turned around to see the computer guy with Jensen. I smiled, and closed the computer's window.

"Just looking."

"You're not on this case, Sergeant," said Jensen. "And neither are you, LeBonte."

"I can help."

"We're calling in the Feds. They have a better contact with the Rosicrucians."

"Are you meaning to tell me that you don't think I'm good enough?" I demanded.

Jenson looked me up and down. "You need a little bit of growing up to do."

"Just because I'm 18 doesn't mean I don't know what I'm doing. I've been through more than you think."

Jensen thumbed us toward the door. "Take him home, Sergeant."

"Yes, sir," said Danny, as he guided me out the door.

We went outside and got in the car.

"I guess I'll be back on patrol," he said.

"Too bad you weren't a detective."

"I'm working on it."

"Need help with that?"

He got in the car on his side before answering. "My mom's working on it."

I held up my hands. "Far be it for me to get in the way of your mom's magic. It'd be more powerful than mine."

He chuckled. "Probably."

We listened to the police chatter as he drove. It was six o'clock when I got home.

Danny watched me get out of the car. "Hey, what's your number?"

I told him my cellular phone number, and he took it down. "I'll call you if I hear anything."

"Great," I said with a smile. "Thanks a lot, Sergeant."

"Don't mention it."

That night, after everyone went to sleep, I found that Angelfire website. On its contact page was an email link and a physical address: a post office box in Providence.

⊛   ⊛   ⊛

"I think I should stay home," I said to Evie as they got ready on Sunday to go to my parents' house.

Evie frowned. "I hate to agree with you, but after last week, I think so, too."

"At least a little while. Until it blows over." I pet Rufus absently. "Can you get mom some flowers for me?"

"Sure."

"I'm going to call Scott, see if I can hang out there."

"Okay."

But first, I was going to go to the post office in Providence.

Taking the bus would have been a complicated maneuver, so I just walked it. The post office itself was open until two, and the area where the post office boxes were located was open later.

I came in before the clerks closed, but I headed to the left, where the boxes were. Number 1757 was a small, rectangular silver square, about the height of a regular business-sized envelope. I had to bend down to look at it.

The box door seemed to bulge. Maybe they didn't pick up their mail that often, and it was full. Well, I'd just have to see.

I spelled the lock open, which was easy enough to do. The door flew open and slammed with a clink against the side of the box to its right.

Then, tendrils of black … magic flowed out of the box, like an octopus or snakes. They wove outward in random directions.

I jumped back, getting out of the way of being touched by the tendrils. I didn't know exactly what they were, but I got the sense they were harmful. I bent down again to peer into the box. All I saw were two envelopes and a small box that could easily hold earrings or a ring.

The tendrils flailed, searching for something to latch onto, but they didn't get any longer than about maybe three inches from the door of the box. I was going to take what was in the box, but I knew that would be a felony — maybe I already was committing one right now. I had to close that box.

I stood next to the side of the box and kicked the door closed. The tendril grabbed a hold of my shoe and sock, but cut off when I closed the door. The tendrils started to fade and disappear. I spelled the lock shut and stood back from the door that again bulged.

And that's when the cop said, "You're under arrest, kid."

ELEVEN

NECROMANCER

"I TOLD YOU," I SAID FOR THE FIFTH OR SIXTH TIME. "I just looked."

"That's still tampering with delivery of the mail, and a federal crime," said the post office guard or police officer or whatever he was.

We had spent a good two hours in an upstairs room, and I had told him I suspected that the owner of the post office box was getting something illegal.

The item that had the tendrils was probably not in itself illegal. It could be to the Rosicrucians,.

"Did you call the detectives I told you to call?"

He said nothing. So, either they hadn't, or the detectives weren't going to help me.

A knock sounded at the door. The guard answered it.

"Finally," he said, and stepped aside.

Two men wearing jackets that said FBI on the back came in. One raised his hand at me.

"Stand up."

I stood up. He came around behind me and handcuffed me. "Hey, wait! Do you read my rights to me or something?"

They shoved me toward the door. I stumbled out of it, down the hall to the elevator.

"Come on, guys. Really?"

I felt along the handcuffs and could feel the hole where the key went in. Easy to spell it open if I had to.

They dragged me out to a black car and shoved me in the back. I hadn't told Scott where I was going and, when Evie and Dom got back, they'd call Scott and find out I wasn't there. I could very well disappear off the face of the earth, and they'd never know.

I found it more nerve-wracking with the silence. They drove through Providence to a big square building that looked like it needed a new coat of glass. When they hauled me out of the back seat, I wondered if I could run away. But they kept their hand on my arm, holding tightly.

They buzzed into the building, onto an elevator to the 17th floor. Down a carpeted hall, through a nondescript door, and into an office.

Chevalier, Reilly's partner, sat there, his hands in a steeple, looking over them at me.

"Thank you, you can leave him here."

The two men left, shutting the door behind them. I heard the click of a lock.

"Take a seat, Grimaulkin."

My God, he knew. "It's kind of hard with these."

He waved a hand and sat back. "Take them off, then."

He knew that too.

I spelled the lock open and the cuffs fell to the floor. I picked them up. He held out his hand.

"You know, I have a lot better things to do on a Sunday afternoon than deal with a rogue."

I dropped the cuffs into his hand. "I thought you weren't a Rosicrucian."

"I'm not. Officially. Are you sure you don't want to become a Knight?"

"I'm absolutely sure."

He said, "I don't blame you. But you can still work for the Rosicrucians without taking the vows."

"Vows? I'd have to take vows?"

"To be a Knight."

"Definitely not, then."

He crossed his arms and sat back. "I had to call in some chips to get you out. You were going to be brought in on murder and other charges. They've been watching that box for days."

"You know what's in that box?"

"We put it there as tracking and bait."

I threw my hands up in frustration. "If you already know, then what's all this with the State Police and the Providence Police and —"

"Everyone has a lack of communication around here. No one wants to work together. They call Rosicrucians in for the really weird stuff, but the city and state and federal police all want to be the ones to say, 'We got the guy.'"

Adults. Worse than three-year-olds.

"Can you give me what information you have and I'll give you what information I have and —"

Chevalier raised his hands. "It's out of my jurisdiction now. It's gone to the FBI. And the FBI have their own Pathfinders."

A Pathfinder was a person who could sense magic coming from a person or place. That's how they were able to find me and arrest me when I summoned Belial over five years before.

"Pathfinders that specialize in detecting Lucifer?"

"Nope. And we don't have time to learn."

"I can learn. Very quickly."

He tightened his grip on his arms, because I saw his shirt stretch out in the shoulders.

"I know a lot of magic. I can do it."

"Last time I talked to you, you couldn't do anything."

"It's different now."

He sat up, and took out his phone. He flipped it open, glancing at it. "Someone just retrieved the stuff in the box."

"So you have someone in custody?" Thinking that they had done the same thing to him that they did to me.

"No." He held the phone to his ear. "Joe. Yeah. Shit." He hung up, glared at me.

"They left the artifact in the trash can at the post office."

"Does it have a residue of the person who touched it?"

"They're examining it now."

Chevalier got up and grabbed his coat from the back of his chair.

"I know a spell that can find them if there is."

"So do the Pathfinders." He picked up the handcuffs and dropped them in an inside pocket. "Let's go."

"Let me help. Please."

"There's nothing you can do."

"What about the guy who was possessed in the hospital?"

"He died this morning."

I raised my head and said the first lie to someone associated with the Rosicrucians. "I can talk to the dead."

He paused at the door. "What?"

I was throwing anything out there, and that popped into my head. I knew a spell that a necromancer from Blackstone taught me, but he was a little crazy, and half of his stuff I didn't believe. If the spell worked — and in theory, it sounded like it could — I would amaze myself. Most importantly, it wasn't Grimalkin's voice that told me I could do this. It was my own.

Most of all, I didn't want to go back to prison.

"I can summon the spirit and talk to the dead."

He threw open the door. "Come on, then."

Every hospital has a morgue, and Chevalier flashed a badge to bring me down to the depths of it. On the way into the hospital, though, I stopped and broke a live foot-long branch off a thin maple tree planted in front of the hospital. At least I had a necromancer's wand.

We got to the morgue, and Chevalier spoke quietly to the orderly there. He brought us into a freezing cold room with bodies stretched out on gurneys. It was cold enough to see our breaths as we walked through.

He stopped at one, checked the wrist band, and then pulled back the sheet.

"We got this," Chevalier said.

The orderly nodded and walked out.

I broke a piece of the branch and handed it to Chevalier. "This will protect you."

"Um, okay."

I raised my hand with the wand and began the chant.

"A-I-E-I-A-O."

It was nonsense, but it built up the energy in my body. I felt the glow in my chest, and forced some of my life force out down my arm, to my hand. I brought my arm down and, closing my eyes, forced life force from my heart into his.

He jerked, like being jolted by a battery, and he sat up. His eyes were open, but black, unseeing.

"Where am I?"

"I command you," I said. "You will not resist."

He turned his head to me, but he didn't see me. "I will not resist."

Chevalier whispered, "Sweet Mary, Jesus, and Joseph."

"What was your name?"

"Roger Bouchard."

"How did Lucifer gain possession of you?"

"We summoned him."

"How many?"

"Seven."

"Where?"

"Providence."

"When?"

"Halloween Eve."

"Seven in a coven?"

"Seven allowed the graces of Lucifer. The Light Bringer. It's so dark."

"Why did you summon Lucifer?"

"His grace. To bless me. For my children. My children."

"Who are the people who summoned Lucifer?"

He gripped the sheet. "Ashmodai. Tabitha. Maurice. Bianca. Richard. Maximillian."

"Who died so far?"

"Bianca and Richard." And himself.

"Where do the rest of them live?"

Roger waved his head from side to side. "Ashmodai was from Newport. Maximillian from Scituate. Tabitha had to come north. Will you send me back?"

I was felt dizzy. I poured my own life energy into him, keeping him "powered up", so to speak.

"Where did he find out about these people?" Chevalier asked, finally regaining his sense of detective work.

"The computer."

"Do you know their last names?"

"No," Bouchard answered. "Will you send me back?"

"I have to," I said. I noticed I was swaying. "I have to."

"It's dark. And cold. He promised."

I pulled the wand away from his heart. He fell backwards onto the table and I stumbled into the gurney behind me, the room spinning.

I think I fell.

I don't know what I smelled, but it made me jerk.

It pulled me out of blackness with a hard jolt. "Oh, my God, what the hell —"

"Smelling salts, works every time," said the orderly.

I was sitting in a puffy chair, while Chevalier stood over me and the orderly sat next to me.

He patted my arm. "All set."

"You okay, Mike?"

I nodded. I looked beyond Chevalier to the windows. It was dark outside.

"What time is it?"

"Six-fifteen."

"I have to get home." I checked my phone. Dead.

"Can you do that again before you go?"

I shook my head. "You can only summon them back once. I didn't know I —"

Chevalier put his hands on his hips. "You didn't know you could do that."

I looked sheepish. "I knew the spell —"

He sighed. "At least we have names."

"I can find them."

"We have Path —"

"But they're not their real names! They're names on the computer. Who walks around with the name Maximillian?"

Chevalier leaned into me. "Mike. With every person that dies, the remaining people get these remaining 'graces'. The last one standing is going to be Lucifer."

"Are you saying that this is going to be dangerous?"

"Now you're getting it."

I stood up slowly. "Bring it on."

Chevalier backed up about a foot.

Finally, he said, "Your goddamn funeral, Mike. I won't be responsible for your death."

"I don't expect to die."

"Your piddly protection spells are probably going to mean nothing."

"Won't know until I try, right?"

"Fine. We'll get Maximillian tonight."

We didn't realize that it was Veteran's Day evening. It was a Saturday, at the beginning of November. The weather was crisp, not freezing.

Scituate is a rural town in the western corner of the state. They have a very proud — and rich — community there. They're also very patriotic.

We certainly didn't realize that Scituate Center was closed for a fireworks display in the local park. People filled the street on both sides. Even with a flashing light on his car, we crawled through the streets.

"We'll have better luck on foot," he said as he pulled into the parking lot of a church. Someone came over to us.

"You gotta move it —"

Chevalier flashed his badge and got out of the car. I got out with him.

The guy was backing up, his hands held up. "Sorry, sir."

"Should we split up?" I asked.

"I can't see if someone's possessed. Can you?"

"Sure," I said. "Do you have sunglasses?"

"Sunglasses. At night?"

Yeah, I thought, that would not only look dumb, but he wouldn't be able to see anything in the dark.

"Scrap that, then. Follow me."

I dove into the crowd. It wasn't a throng, so there was space between people to move around. The crowd did get thicker as we headed toward the field where the fireworks would go off from.

Then I smelled it: the iron-sweet smell of sulfur.

I stayed still and looked around, catching the eye of people, glancing at their aura. One large man stood two layers deep away from me. He wore glasses, had a black hoodie on under his jean jacket, and glared at me with such an intense hatred that I felt the hackles on the back of my neck stand up.

Then he raised his hand and a ball of hellfire shot out from his palm.

It missed me, but got the baby stroller next to me. The stroller burst into flame, the mother screamed, Chevalier came out of nowhere to dive into the fray. I ignored all of it, focusing on the man, who turned to try and lose himself in the crowd.

I saw him, scented him, and shoved my way through to follow. He looked back to see me gaining, and he shot off another ball of fire. This time, I was ready, and yelled out the protective shield spell. It hit the shield, just inches above the heads of everyone in a ten-foot radius. The effect was a wave of fire on a bubble above everyone.

When the flame dissipated after hitting my shield, I dove after him again. He got to an area where there were less people, and I had more room to pour on speed. I tackled him, knocking him to the ground.

"I will kill you, mage," he growled, as the hoodie fell from his head.

He had horns in his hair. Curved, black horns.

He tried to wiggle out from under me, but I moved back. When I did, I fell off of him. I expected him to get up.

Instead, he went into convulsions. He started foaming at the mouth, choking. I turned his head, or tried to, and he vomited writhing white worms in thick, dark bile. I pulled my hands away and the man, Maximillian, stopped moving.

A crowd had gathered, and I scrambled up, off the dead man, before Lucifer could jump into me. I had the nagging thought that could happen, because that's what demons did when their hosts died. But Chevalier said that because the cult had summoned him, the demon would return to the cult.

And make each one of them more powerful.

"Chevalier!" I yelled, and ran back into the crowd.

I broke through a ring of people, where first responders were already there. Someone was on a gurney, heading into an ambulance. The charred remains of twisted metal, plastic, and burnt nylon lie in the center of the street. A woman with burnt arms sat on a curb crying, a man with his arms around her, and a rescue person trying to talk to her.

I dashed toward the gurney, but a cop stopped me.

"Where you goin', kid?"

I had to think fast to get into that ambulance. I screamed, "That's my father. I lost him in the crowd."

The cop glanced back at the ambulance. "Go, quick."

I ran to the ambulance just as they were going to shut the doors.

"Dad!" I yelled.

"We don't have time for passengers," said the paramedic, and shut the door.

"I'll take you," said a Scituate cop. "They're going to Rhode Island."

Rhode Island Hospital. I knew that place well.

The Scituate cop got me into a car and we barreled down Route 195 to get to Providence. We had to go through some back streets to get to the hospital, but we pulled into the Emergency Room entrance just as the gurney was getting unloaded.

The sheet covered his face.

TWELVE

THE REMAINS

I ENDED UP TELLING THE STORY TO FIVE PEOPLE: Reilly, Dom and Evie, Scott, and now, the Confessor.

"How did you feel?" The Confessor asked me when I sat in his office.

"How did *I* feel?"

He was the first person who asked me how I felt after I finished telling the story. I was surprised by the question.

"Well, sad, I guess."

"How did you express it? Did you cry?"

"No."

"Did you punch the wall?"

"No. I just kinda … I stood there until another car came by and I had to move out of the way."

"Then what did you do?"

"I stayed there until Reilly showed up."

"Have you cried at all, Mike?"

I remembered last night, before going to sleep. Hearing Chevalier's voice as he told me he had better things to do. Seeing him rush into the flames. Smelling the burnt flesh, even though I wasn't near him enough to actually smell it.

Did I whimper on the couch last night, or was that Rufus?

"No," I said in a firm, but angry tone.

The Confessor tilted his head. "All right," he said. "But you felt nothing?"

"I said I felt sad."

"You guess."

"I don't remember. All right?"

"All right, Mike."

We sat for a minute in silence. Then I said, "I felt lost. Overwhelmed. Confused. What do I do now? This is *Lucifer*."

"Mike, you know how to summon and banish demons."

"Lesser demons. Dukes, kings, earls, commanders of legions."

"Lucifer is still a demon, and has his own binding angels. You know who cast him out of heaven, don't you?"

"Michael," I muttered.

"You can beat him."

"Grimalkin's afraid of him."

"You don't need Grimalkin." He pointed to his own head. "You have everything you need right here."

I might have had everything in my head, but it was the fear that roiled in my guts. Chevalier said the last man standing was going to be the most powerful.

"I can't do this by myself," I said.

"What do you want, a magic sword? A secret amulet? You know what happens in those stories — the power is within the person. You have the ability, the will, and the determination."

"People are going to die."

"Even if the Rosicrucians did this on their own, people would die. The cult members are going to die, no matter what. They should have known this before going in."

"So I'm some kind of avenger?"

"If you want to look at it that way." He rose. "This is what you're made for, Mike."

I didn't get up at first. I didn't feel as confident as he seemed to feel about me. I was going to screw up; I knew I was.

He held his hand out to me. "Trust me, Mike."

I refused his hand and got up from the chair.

"Every time someone says that, I get screwed."

Scott saw me slink into the store while he talked to two college kids.

"Reading cards is easy. You learn a few key words to the cards, and you can weave a story with them."

"Don't you need to be a psychic?"

"Not necessarily."

While he talked to them, I took down some herbs and sniffed them. The deep, earthy smell of patchouli helped me to think.

Did I really have to do this? Did I really have to hunt down Lucifer, or whoever was going to be Lucifer? Most likely it would be that man Ashmodai.

I thought about Chevalier. I couldn't even remember his last words to me. His last action was to try to save the baby from the hellfire. He didn't succeed. Why did he try? He wasn't a Knight. He had no magical protection. He just jumped in.

Then what did I do? Run after the guy. Who died. What was the worth in that? I could have saved Chevalier. Could I? If … if … if …

Scott put his hand on my shoulder, startling me out of my thoughts. I was still inhaling the patchouli from the jar.

"Are you okay?" he asked me.

I closed the jar and put it back. "Thinking about last night."

"I'm sorry," he said, stepping away.

I took his hand and turned around to face him. I held his hand to my chest, bending my head to kiss his knuckles. "Would you have tried to save a baby if it was on fire?"

"Probably," he said. "But that's the type of person I am."

"I didn't. I went after the demon."

"But you saved those other people when he tried to set them on fire, too."

There was that.

"And you stopped him from causing any more harm."

I sighed. "But a good man died."

"Mike, he was a cop. He tried to save a person because that's what cops do. Just ask Frank."

I didn't let go of Scott's hand.

He placed his other hand on top of mine. "You saved people. You're a good man, too, Mike."

We stayed there for a while like that. I don't cry easily; crying is not something I do anymore. It was beaten out of me in prison. You don't show weakness. Instead, I let it sit there, like a rock in my stomach, not allowing it to rise up to my eyes. I kept my head bent, feeling the heat of his hands on my lips and in my hands.

Finally, I let him go with a light kiss on his lips. "Can I come over tonight? I have tomorrow off."

"I open late on Tuesdays. I guess you can come over."

I laughed. "You guess?"

"Unless you get called out for something else again."

"Maybe I should shut off my phone."

"They'll find you."

"Is that a prediction?"

"Let's hope not. I want to spend time with you."

That rock in my stomach dissolved in that very instant. It turned into something warm and fuzzy — a curled-up purring cat on my lap, something that caused me to exhale slowly. My happy sigh followed him when he went to the back room to get me a soda.

Three were left.

I lay in Scott's bed, staring up at the cracks in the ceiling, while Scott lay across my chest, still sleeping. I was wide awake at the sunrise, with the thought of: *There are three left.*

Three.

Three is a magic number.

Lucifer was going to be powerful if all three were in one place. Ashmodai was the leader.

I needed the *Grimorum Verium*. Scott didn't have a copy. I would have to go to DeLuna's place in Salem — unless the Rosicrucians would let me use the library. I could offer them the fact that I was doing all this work for them, and that I needed the grimoire to complete the work. My memory depended on Grimalkin, and he wasn't being reliable.

Besides the fact that Grimalkin *was* my memory — if what the Confessor said was true.

Three left — three people with Lucifer's "graces". Lucifer could give a lot of different blessings as an angel, according to my memory. Most of those blessings had to do with power and authority. But since Lucifer was the head of all demons, he could assume any form, bestow any blessings, that the conjurer would want.

The obvious were the seven deadly sins.

Wait just a second.

I felt my body stiffen as things clicked in my mind.

Seven members of the cult.

Seven deadly sins.

I moved my fingers as I whispered them, "Lust, envy, greed, gluttony, wrath, pride …"

"Sloth," said Scott while he still lay on my chest.

"You're awake," I said, looking down at him.

"Mmmhmmm." He stirred and looked up at me. "Wondering which of the deadly sins we haven't done yet?"

"No. It just came to me. Seven cult members were involved in summoning Lucifer. Could it be one for each?"

"You know, that could be."

"The guy I chased after in Scituate was possibly gluttony, because he was a big guy. The boy who killed his parents could be envy, wrath, or even greed."

"You don't know who belongs to what sin. Who's left?"

"Ashmodai, who I would guess is pride if he took the name of one of the most powerful demons. Some girl named Tabitha, and … dammit, I forgot."

Scott traced the lines of my chest and abdomen with his finger as he spoke. "Maybe you should call and find out?"

"I thought you wanted to spend time with me."

"I do. But I know you too well. This will eat at you until you solve it."

I looked down at his red hair. "You did a good job of distracting me last night, though."

He put his arms on my chest and lay his head on his hands, gazing into my eyes. "I can't be a constant distraction."

I rubbed his back. "Sure you can."

He chuckled and rolled off me. "Call Reilly and find out what's going on."

He got out of bed and slipped on a pair of knit boxers on his way to the bathroom.

I sighed. Scott did know me too well. I leaned over the bed and fished my phone out of my pants and turned it on.

It seemed Reilly had been trying to get a hold of me, because there was a call at 2:30 in the morning from his number. Good thing I had shut the phone off, or I wouldn't have been, ah … distracted.

I called the number. He answered after two rings. "Where the hell you been?"

"Sleeping, like normal people," I said, sitting up. Scott came back into the room. "What's going on?"

"Do you know about something called a Grimaulkin?"

I sat bolt upright, my whole body tensing up. I distinctly heard the "u", but I asked him to spell it. He did, and it had the "u" in it.

"Yes," I said. "It's me."

"Somebody left you a message."

"Where?"

"Cumberland Monastery."

I had been there to get my wand and staff, way back when I was first released from prison and had to banish Belial. I only claimed dead tree branches. I figured my essence had left the place since April, and it was November now.

"Can you bring me there?"

"Where are you?"

"I'll meet you at the same coffee shop that —"

"Thayer?"

"Yeah."

"Be there in ten minutes."

He hung up, and I looked at Scott, who sat next to me on the bed. I told him that there was a message for me at the Cumberland Monastery.

"That doesn't sound good," said Scott.

I got dressed quickly. "No. No, it doesn't."

"Will you promise me something?"

I turned to him. "Anything," I said, my voice thick and quiet.

"Be careful." He took my hands in his.

"Do you know something?"

"A feeling. It's not clear. It's just a feeling. Please be careful."

"I will," I said, giving him a long, full kiss.

I walked down to Thayer. As I headed to the coffee house, I heard a beep of a horn, and saw Reilly's car. He double-parked as I stood at the passenger side door. I hesitated.

"Get in, will you?"

I got in, buckled my seat belt. He turned down Waterman and ended up going back down to Pawtucket.

"Can you stop at the library?" I asked. I wondered if they would have left me a message in my usual spot.

"Don't have time for that."

"When we come back?"

"If they're open."

I guessed that would have to do. We went around Pawtucket, into Cumberland, to the Monastery grounds — which was also the Cumberland library. Reilly parked before a small bridge that looked rickety which led to a playground. No other police cars seemed to be in the area.

He lifted the yellow tape around a couple of trees, and we walked a few feet to a well-built yellow stage that needed a paint job. It especially needed one because of what was spray-painted on the stage in red letters outlined in black: "We & coming GRIMAULKIN." Beneath that was a black circle with red letters spelling out "SATAN" along its circumference.

"Obviously doesn't have a good command of the English language," said Reilly.

"That's not what I'm worried about," I said, pointing to the sigils. "These letters. They don't have the complete circle around them."

I bent down and touched the "S". There was no power coming from it.

"Which means?"

"The spell is incomplete. It's just for show." I straightened up. "Someone's trying to scare me."

"'Trying' is the operative word here, right?" asked Reilly.

"What I don't get is how do they know my name? He called me Michael before." The magic world was a small one, and wizards ran into each other all the time. "I've only been here six months."

"Maybe there's a mole in the police?"

I tilted my head at him.

"You've helped us out a lot. Chevalier was getting close to something. Maybe he tripped a wire."

"Tripped a wire?"

"Said something to the wrong person and started a chain of events to get you involved."

"This is my *prison* name," I said, pointing with my foot to my name. "I never told Chevalier. Or anybody." Unless, again, my name was known among magicians and demons.

Reilly walked around the area. "I'm going to let them know that they can come and paint it over now."

I nodded. Reilly walked off the stage; I stayed on it. I stepped in the circle, sensing no power there. It wasn't even a trap.

"Who wants me?"

I closed my eyes. Because no energy was put into the construction of the circle or the letters, I couldn't tell who did what. I couldn't replay the essence of the moment, either.

I heard a dog howl.

I opened my eyes, but nothing in the area had changed. I stepped out of the circle, onto my name, closing my eyes again.

The howl.

I kept my eyes closed and concentrated on the howl.

"Come to me," I commanded.

It got louder. I heard breathing, panting. I squeezed my eyes shut, not looking. The direction it came from was right in front of me.

Without warning, I punched outward and connected. I opened my eyes, but nothing was there. I had felt the connection with my fist: I had hit something.

Then something relatively light hit me in the back of the head, and I stumbled forward. I righted myself, turning to face what was behind me. The forest area beyond the stage shimmered, like looking through a window covered with falling rain. I punched again. It connected and the shimmering ducked to one side.

Stepping on the "T" on the circle, I let my body sense where the essence was, leaning on my boxing training from prison. I sensed something coming at me from the left. I pivoted, reached out with both hands, and thrust my hands into the shimmering area.

I grabbed fur and twisted, throwing it down. It fell on top of the word "We", blurring the word beneath it. I kicked hard. I felt the connection and heard the snapping of bones, and then the thing appeared.

A large black lab, not dissimilar to Rufus, lay for a moment on top of the "We". Its eyes blazed with fire, but it went out seconds before the creature disappeared.

Panting, I backed up away from the circle to the edge of the stage. Nothing remained of the fight but my rapidly beating heart.

THIRTEEN

BREAK STUFF

I DIDN'T TELL REILLY ABOUT THE FIGHT, such as it was. I wasn't even sure it had happened.

He dropped me off at the Pawtucket library. I immediately checked my "mail", but nothing was there. Then I went to the gym.

I summoned a change of clothes from home into a locker that I used in an emergency for teleporting clothes. I had etched the sigils into the paint of the locker so it was permanent. At least until — or if — they painted over them.

After a workout and a swim, it was past time for lunch. I changed into new clothes and went to Scott's store.

He hadn't opened. I found that odd, but not unusual. He did say he was going to open late, but late for him was noontime.

I hung around the store for about fifteen minutes, then called him. He didn't answer his phone, so I left a message, telling him I was at the store.

I waited another fifteen minutes, called again. Maybe he forgot his phone at home and was out somewhere getting new stock. I left him another message saying I was heading home.

As I headed up Main Street, a trooper pulled alongside me.

"Hey, Sergeant Costa," I said, when I poked my head in the passenger's side.

"Hey, Mike. We got a lead."

I jumped in. "What's going on?"

Lights blared and he cut people off as he got on the highway.

"Ashmodai's moving."

"You know who he is?"

"We know *where* he is."

"Where?"

"Newport. Did you know that all computers have their own address?"

"I didn't know."

"We found Ashmodai's. We were monitoring Roger's AOL and he got an email this morning. The FBI traced it back to his computer."

"The FBI?"

"And your buddies: the Rosicrucians."

"Are they going to even let us near the place?"

He grinned. "We'll find out when we get there."

I hung on for the ride.

We blasted across the Newport Bridge and squealed into downtown Newport, where we ended up in a bottleneck around Long Wharf. Part of the street was blocked off by local police.

Costa parked the car in the middle of the street. I got a sick sense of *deja vu* — like when Chevalier had parked the car and we walked together into the mess that was Scituate. In this case, there cars blocked the cobblestone street in a fifty-yard radius, in front of a pair of houses: one with columns, one without.

Costa strode through the area like he owned it. No one stopped us until we got to the FBI ring, when one man put a hand on Costa's chest, stopping him.

He stepped aside and I came into view. The guy was classic FBI, clean-cut, suit and tie, dark glasses.

"You look awful young to be the Rosicrucian's necromancer."

I didn't even bother to look at Costa. "Don't judge a book by its cover."

The agent took me by the elbow, leading me away from Costa. I hoped to God that Costa wouldn't end up dead.

He brought me to a command center — or at least I guessed it was, since there was a knot of FBI and Rosicrucians there. I could tell the Rosicrucians because their magic was palatable — I could literally taste it in the air.

"You're a necromancer?" one of them asked me.

"Sure," I said.

'Who's your mentor?"

"I don't need a mentor."

The Rosicrucians looked at each other. I felt them building up their magic to test me.

I stepped away from the group and walked around the parked car they gathered around, going out to the cobblestone street, across from the white house with the columns.

"Get him out of there!" I heard someone yell, but I kept walking to the base of the house, onto the sidewalk across from the parked car.

"Hey, Ashmodai. Asmodeus."

The door burst open. A man the size of a small bull came running out. However, he tripped down the uneven granite stairs and ended up sprawling flat at my feet.

I danced back into the street. The man got up, his face red from blood and fury. I assumed a smaller boxing stance, the first stance I had learned when I was still a pre-teen, keeping myself compact and tight.

The man roared and swung out at me. I moved back. He had arms as thick as my legs, and a long reach. I'd have to duck in and hit him quick before he could grab me.

But he wasn't fighting me strategically. He was straight out brawling, flailing his arms and legs to try and hit me. I almost tripped over one cobblestone higher than the rest, and got onto the sidewalk, which was brick. My back was to the house, and his back was to the Rosicrucians.

I had never seen the Rosicrucians fight magic. I saw three men break out from behind the car and take positions to create a circle around him.

However, I was the center of the bastard's attention. I had to keep myself out of his way because one of those ham-fists to my face — or any part of my body — looked like he could break it.

I moved side to side, while the other three magicians did their dance at the same time, keeping themselves at an exact distance from each other and me. They said the spell. I didn't know it, so I couldn't join in; not that I was really concentrating on that.

I tripped on a brick, cursing authenticity over utility, and fell in the monster's reach. He roared with triumph and headed right for me. I let myself fall down and rolled sideways into the street. He hit me on the shoulder, but not half as hard as I expected. I pulled myself into a fetal position, protecting my head, and I heard a loud bang: metal hitting metal.

Then a thud.

I lifted my head to see the man passed out next to me. An FBI agent came up to him with cuffs, but one of the Rosicrucians waved him away. Another Rosicrucian showed up and started drawing a circle around the large, prone body.

I got to my feet, backing up out of the way of the circle. I knew it was a banishment circle, and they didn't care that the man inside it was going to live or die.

The Rosicrucians joined hands, making a triangle around the circle. They spoke in Hebrew; I knew some of the words, but not the details. I knew it was a banishment.

The man in the circle arched his back and screamed. I could see a black shadow escape from his mouth and fly upward, through the window of the house.

This wasn't Ashmodai. This was Wrath.

A shot rang out and a piece of brick near one man's foot exploded.

I ran to the house, through the open doors and inside. The house smelled like wood oil and musty carpets. From what I could see in the dim light, the decorations were of an 1800's nautical theme.

I stalked through the rooms on the bottom floor, looking for stairs leading up. *What the hell was I doing?*

What I should have done for Chevalier.

The rooms had 1800's gilded mirrors over mantles, watercolors of ships from the age of sail, dark mahogany wood paneling and furniture. None of it looked comfortable; it felt like walking through a museum.

Finally, I found a set of stairs at the back of the house, and followed them up. Although the walls were still dark, the smell was more lived-in, not thick and cloying like downstairs. I kept looking for stairs.

I heard another gunshot from outside. Ashmodai was sniping from somewhere above.

Moving faster, I found more stairs. These led to lighter rooms — rooms painted white and blue, with comfortable chairs and couches. Some doors were closed, and I left them that way.

I found a trap door open with a set of stairs leading up. Obviously, this would lead to an attic. I put one foot on the step and was thrown face forward into the steps as something attacked me from behind.

It bit into my left shoulder, and I yelped in pain. I tried to roll to the side to get it off, but it held onto my shoulder. I fell off the stairs to the hardwood floor, the thing on my back, claws digging into my back as the animal held on.

I rolled again, trying to get to my hands and knees. It was heavy. I felt its growl as it pulled out a chunk of meat from my left shoulder — the shoulder that Scott and the Rosicrucians had healed after Belial shot it. I imagined for a moment I had a target there.

It was off-center for a half-second, so I threw myself upward, to try and vault it over my head. Blood from the wound arced over my head to the floor and the creature, a giant black lab, followed the blood splatter.

All I could think of was: *Now Lucifer has my blood.*

I didn't notice that my arm buckled beneath my weight. The dog scrambled to its feet. I got to mine, ignoring the flow of blood down my arm dripping to the floor.

The dog growled and jumped at me. I swung at his head with my right hand, intending a right hook. Like fighting the invisible dog in the Monastery, it connected, and it hit hard. I felt bones crack in my hand and its jaw seemed to disconnect from his head. When it landed, barely on its feet, its bottom jaw was a good three inches dislocated from its upper jaw. It tried to close its mouth, but it couldn't; its tongue lolled out sideways.

It stumbled, whining. Its eyes weren't on fire; it wasn't a hellhound. I had just punched a poor dog's lights out. Considering how I felt about the dogs in the breeders, I felt horrible.

"Sorry, puppy,"

I went back to the stairs, glancing back. The dog fell at the bottom step. Then I looked at my arm, soaked in blood. I grabbed the rope with my right hand and guided myself up the stairs.

It led to an attic, and right before me a door was open to the fresh air outside. I stepped through it, finding myself on a three-foot wide ledge that wrapped the very top of the house. I started walking around it. Then I saw Ashmodai.

I expected a white-haired robed wizard, with a goatee and mustache, about fifty years old or better, fit and trim and ready for fighting.

One out of four preconceived notions was pretty bad.

He was blond, wearing a baseball cap backwards, dressed in woodsman-camouflage, thick hiking boots, with a bolt-action rifle pointing through the slats of the railing around the widows' walk. He was fit and trim, but he was in his thirties, or maybe even a little less.

He looked up at me, his eyes red with fire.

He grinned. "Come join me, Michael."

"Not here for that," I said, and kicked the gun out of his hands. It jammed through the slats, hanging off the edge.

He reached and grabbed my ankle, yanking me down with a strength that normal men didn't have. I fell hard on my injured shoulder. I howled, kicked at Ashmodai's face with my free foot, but he grabbed it.

With the strength he had, he could easily swing me over the railing by my ankles. So I grabbed a hold of a slat and held on with both hands, though my left hand was slick with blood and couldn't grip well. I felt him pulling my legs, thinking this was how a medieval rack would feel, with my joints getting yanked out. I wouldn't let him get that far.

I relaxed, giving him the sense that he was winning. He loosened his grip as I expected.

I kicked him in the face.

He jerked back, letting me go, both hands going to his nose, and I pulled myself away. He scrambled back, getting to his feet, still holding onto his nose.

"I'll kill you, mage!"

Then his head exploded. It only took one shot from someone on the ground to take him out.

I lost whatever was left of my breakfast over the side of the house.

I heard someone yelling, "Don't shoot!", and thought I could hear boots on the wood.

One remained.

FOURTEEN

ALMOST GONE

I WAS NEVER GOING TO MAKE IT AS A COP if I kept losing my lunch over the sight of exploded body parts.

The paramedics cleaned me up. I had a gouge of flesh out of my shoulder. I had lost a lot of blood, and was supposedly in shock because I walked downstairs to the rescue on my own power.

I could get to Scott and he would heal me up. In the meantime, I was heading to Rhode Island Hospital. I lay in the gurney, concentrating through the painkillers they gave me. I could heal myself in a limited manner, but Scott was the true healer out of both of us.

When I got to Rhode Island, Evie was there, waiting.

"What happened?" she asked as she followed the paramedics and me.

"He's a hero," said the paramedic.

"Nah," I said. "Just crazy."

"Is that your shirt?"

I looked down at my shirt, cut up in a pile at my lap. It was crusty with dried blood.

"Um, it was."

"Do you want to walk to the bed?" asked the paramedics.

"Sure," I said. I waited until they put the gurney down, and swung my legs to the side.

The room spun, and the next thing I knew, I was in the bed, throwing up in a bucket again.

Dom had appeared suddenly. "What happened to your shoulder?"

"Dog bite."

"Some dog."

I laughed so hard I threw up again.

The doctors decided to keep me. They would get a specialist to see if they could get someone to work on my shoulder. I told them I heal myself.

They were all, "Yeah, right. Let's put you on the psych ward instead."

I had to wait until late at night, when they got me in a room with three old snoring people. I refused the pain medication, refused the sleeping medication, and waited until an hour or so after shift change.

I was in pain, there was no doubt. I was exhausted, and I was sorely tempted on calling upon an entity to heal me. But that was against my parole. Not to mention that entity would probably take one of these old men with him as payment.

Getting out of bed was a painful experience, even while I was attached to the IV. I couldn't draw a circle. I couldn't reach around the bed.

Across from the bed was a marker and a white board that had the name of the nurse written on it in case I needed it. I stretched as far as I could, my fingertips touching the edge of the marker. It rolled off the ledge to the floor.

I swore and reached out with my foot this time. I rolled the marker toward me and was finally able to reach it.

Blue. *How appropriate.*

Blue: the color of water, the element of healing.

I went back to my bed and pulled up the sheet. I drew a circle on the sheet and a sigil of the angel of healing. I wasn't summoning the entity, just the energy. At least that's what I would tell the Rosicrucians if they asked.

I folded the sheet sixteen times, into a neat packet, and redrew the circle in a smaller area. Then I tore off the bandage they put on my back, wincing as I yanked the scabs off. I placed the sheet against my back, and lay back in bed.

Casting my head back, I panted at the exertion. But I felt the water flow into the wound.

Or maybe it was my blood pouring out of it.

Whatever it was, I fell asleep with it.

The doctors let me go the next morning, scratching their heads at how I could have healed so quickly. I didn't have much strength in my left hand because the muscles hadn't gotten strong enough, but they were rebuilt, thanks to the angel's help.

Scott hadn't called me. Evie said that she hadn't seen Scott in the store, either. I had Evie drive by his house.

His truck wasn't in the driveway, or on the few streets that he typically parked. We drove by the store, and it was still closed. I stopped at the Coffee Cup, and Chris listened to me tell him I was in the hospital. I would be in work in the morning, barring anything strange.

I kept calling Scott. Now, I was getting worried. Evie had taken the day off with me.

"Stop calling him, Mike," she said, when I picked up the phone for the third time that hour.

"This isn't like him."

"Maybe Frank knows?"

I called him.

"I was gonna ask you," Frank said. "I haven't seen him in three days."

One day I could account for, because he was with me. "This isn't like him," I said. "I'm going to his house."

I told Evie where I was going. As I walked out of the house, I saw Ritter's car across the street.

Well, there was nothing for it. I approached him. He rolled down the window on his side.

"Do I have an appointment?" I asked.

"With the devil. Get in."

"I just got straightened out, and now you —"

"Get used to it, Grimaulkin." He turned onto the highway. "You work for the Rosicrucians; you're on call all the time."

"What makes you think I'm working for you?"

"You started this," he said. "You're going to finish it."

I sighed. Just when I could lift a frying pan with my left hand, I was going back into battle again. And I wasn't ready. My boyfriend was out there somewhere.

"Dammit, Ritter, I have —"

He gave me a steady look while going seventy miles an hour.

"Watch the road!"

He took his hands off the wheel.

"Ritter!"

He slowly turned back to the road. The car turned on its own, avoiding a truck.

We got off in Warwick, at the airport. "We know she's trying to get away." Ritter said.

"She? Nobody said anything about a 'she'."

"It's Lucifer, Grimaulkin, not a woman."

He parked right in front of the entrance, along a line of other black cars and vans: the Rosicrucians and FBI.

"Fan out," Ritter said. "He'll be coming for you. We'll keep you in our sights."

I walked into the airport alone, trying to look nonchalant. I didn't do a good job, scanning the area and seeing agents and Rosicrucians with everyone in a dark suit. I walked past the luggage check in, into the terminal.

I stood in the center of the terminal, exhaling sharply, to try and get some calming into me. Which direction would Lucifer be in?

Then I said, "I want to join you, Lucifer."

I felt a mental tug to the left. I turned that way and walked down the carpeted terminal. Glass enclosed me on both sides after I passed a few shops.

Then a woman stepped out of the bathroom and stopped right in front of me. She wore a green velvet short dress, black high heels, carrying a small purse. She had long black hair, deep brown skin, and looked absolutely stunning enough to turn every man's head, even mine.

She pursed her lips and gave me a kiss, pressing her body against mine. Her body heat covered me; her smell of jasmine went right to my head, the velvet of her dress soft and giving under my touch.

"Come with me," she said.

I was under a spell. I followed like a dutiful puppy.

Lust, dammit. She's Lust!

I dug my heels in, forcing myself to come to a stop.

She turned around and faced me. "You will not change your mind now, will you, Michael?"

"You're not my type."

Her grin was totally malicious.

Glass shattered all around us. People screamed, and I ducked behind a pillar while spears of glass pierced the area I had been in. I got a thick shard of glass in my calf, going through it.

Thankfully missing any arteries.

However, it still made me stumble and hang onto the pillar. She slunk her way through the shards of glass to my side.

"Ah, Michael. Such a powerful wizard, yet such a weak mind."

She raised her hand: a long spear of glass appeared in it. She aimed it at my eye.

"I banish you in the name of Yahweh."

She laughed. "As if that —"

I knocked the shard of glass out of her hand, and gave her a hard shove to the floor. She wasn't a woman. She was Lucifer.

She fell onto glass, and suddenly three burly men started running toward me. I picked up a piece of glass. "I banish you."

She seemed to think that the men would make it before I completed my motion.

"I banish you!" I yelled, and thrust downward, at the same time the men slammed into me.

I didn't get her heart. The three guys punched me relentlessly. Other men started showing up. I pulled myself into a fetal position to protect important parts, but I kept getting kicked and punched over and over. I repeated the spell to create the protective shield around me.

I felt the shield rise up, and the punches became less and less painful. Then they stopped all together.

Someone tapped my shoulder. It was Ritter.
"You okay?"
"Uh huh," I said, though I felt like a broken toy.
"She's dead."
I rested my head on the shattered glass. It was over.
Finally.

FIFTEEN

SCOTT

After the Rosicrucians in the field healed me up, I still felt sore everywhere. It was after six when I had Ritter drop me off at Scott's. The lights were off in his apartment.

I unlocked the door downstairs with a simple spell and climbed to the third floor. In the dark, I was able to spell his door open. I went inside his apartment.

It stunk of old food. He always washed his dishes after eating. I went to the kitchen and found dirty dishes stacked in standing water in the sink.

I checked his bowl by the door and saw his keys were gone, but his wallet was there. He never went anywhere without his wallet.

The hackles on the back of my neck went up, and my breath came faster.

Something was wrong. Definitely wrong. I felt my heartbeat quicken. My mind went through what could have happened. Did he go for a quick drive and crash somewhere? Was he in the hospital?

Worst of all, did someone beat him up because they found out he was gay? I had heard horrible things people did to gay men: from dragging them around led on the back of a truck to beating them and dumping their body in the nearest river.

"Calm, Mike. You can't do anything if you panic," I said to myself.

I took a few deep breaths, raising my hands up to chest level, then slowly pushing them down, pushing down the panic to my solar plexus, where I could draw on its energy if I needed.

Then I got the idea of a location spell. I had never done one on Scott before. I forced myself to calmly walk into his bathroom. I searched for his comb and brush. But he was clean about that, too, having taken the hair off them after I told him that people could use hair for malevolent sympathetic magic.

I checked his electric razor, opening the compartment and pouring out some of the bits of skin and hair into my palm. I needed something to put it in.

I remembered he had an inventory closet, so I searched through there, digging out a small velvet satchel. I slipped what was in my palm into the satchel and tied it.

"Where are you?"

I tossed it in the air, and it fell to the floor.

I'm panicking, I thought.

I threaded the satchel through a piece of twine, and then swung the item like a pendulum. But it went around and around in a circle.

According to that, I was over him.

Again, my mind went directly to the worst-case scenario: *What if he was buried in the cellar?*

"Oh, my God!"

I burst through the door, barreling headlong down the stairs. The cellar door was locked. I pulled the handle so hard I yanked it off the door.

I backed up and ran into the door with my good shoulder, but it didn't budge. I slammed into it again, this time crashing through it. I tumbled down the wooden stairs, slamming into the stone foundation at their end, before they curved and three steps hit the dirt floor of the cellar.

"Scott!"

I thought I could hear scuffling. Mice? Rats?

"Scott!" I held the satchel and it swung ahead of me.

Then I definitely heard a high-pitched muffled sound.

I followed the satchel and came to an old plywood door with a hole for a handle. I opened the door and cupped my hand over my solar plexus, pulling out energy for a light.

In the pale white light that I generated, I saw Scott in only a pair of dirty shorts, handcuffed and tied spread-eagle on an exposed steel spring mattress, with gray duct tape across his mouth. He turned his head toward me, his eyes wide.

"Oh, God."

I let the light suspend in the air as I untied his legs and went to work on his hands.

"Well, it took you long enough."

I turned at the voice.

The man filled the door frame, the light reflecting off the zippers on his black motorcycle jacket.

"Malachi."

He chuckled. "Some love."

I spelled open the handcuffs while Malachi stood there. I at least had enough presence of mind to do that simple spell. However, Scott still had the duct tape around his mouth.

"I knew something was wrong when his wallet was still there."

Malachi snapped his fingers. "It's been a while since I've done a kidnapping. Give a guy a break."

"What do you want?" I said.

"You dead."

Malachi came into the room. "You know what you did? You destroyed my reputation."

"Oh, poor baby," I said.

"They wanted to join *you*. You — a little shrimpy kid who hallucinated."

I could see out of the corner of my eye that Scott sat up, rubbing his wrists. I kept my eyes on Malachi.

Malachi pulled out a butterfly knife, flicking it open. He grinned, and rushed at me.

Both Scott and I ran to opposite ends of the room. Malachi turned in my direction, totally underestimating Scott. Scott had been in a military boarding school. Scott knew how to fight as well as me.

I ducked sideways. Malachi went that way, and Scott pounced. He wrapped his legs around Malachi's waist. He tucked his arms under Malachi's armpits and threw his weight back, pulling Malachi down, off balance, to the floor. The butterfly knife flew away into the dark. I jumped on Malachi's stomach with both feet while Scott let go of his waist.

Malachi exhaled sharply. I knew I had ruptured something, but I didn't care. I knelt over him.

I felt all the rage — over the whole years, over the last few days, everything ... punch after punch until Scott pulled me off him.

My knuckles were broken and bloody; his face was a mess. But he was alive.

Score one for me.

SIXTEEN

NEWS

"I UNDERSTOOD THAT THEY THREW AWAY MALACHI'S KEY," said the Confessor.

I nodded. "How he got past the Confessors, I don't know."

"We're investigating."

We were silent for a minute.

"So," I said. "Do I need to still see you?"

"You haven't seen Grimalkin in a month, and you've remembered most of your spells without him, and you're working … I'd guess you're in a good place."

I got up.

He got up with me. "I hope to not see you again under such circumstances. But pop by anytime."

I smiled and shook his hand. "Thanks."

I went out to waiting room. Ritter stood up when I entered.

"He's discharged," said the Confessor.

The left side of Ritter's lips quirked upward. "All right."

We got out to the car.

He turned to me. "Don't think this means that I'm not going to keep an eye on you."

"I still have to see my parole officer every so often, right? You'll be taking me to see him, I'm sure."

"Be sure of that, Grimaulkin."

"Mike. Call me Mike."

He looked at me up and down. "Mike."

He drove me to Scott's store. Strangely enough, Evie and Dom were there. I wondered why.

I walked in, and I must have had this confused look on my face, because Evie said, "Mikey! Guess what?"

"What?"

"We found a house!"

"East Providence," said Dom. "There's an in-law apartment for you and Scott."

"Me and Scott?"

"Sure."

I looked at Scott.

He blushed. "We haven't really talked about that," Scott said.

"And guess what else?" Evie put her arms around my neck and gazed with a twinkle into my eyes.

"Um …"

"You're going to be an uncle!"

ABOUT THE AUTHOR

Find out more about the world of L. A. Jacob at
Grimalkin's Grimoire (grimaulkin.com) and
Dark Mystic Quill (darkmysticquill.com)

YOU MIGHT ALSO ENJOY

GRIMAULKIN

by L. A. Jacob

*Treading the straight and narrow is not natural
to one who summons demons.*

GRIMAULKIN TEMPTED

by L. A. Jacob

*Stress affects people differently. Then, there's
magic.*

HOMECOMING
A War Mage Novel

by Jake Logan

*Even wizards in the U.S. armed forces have to go
home some time.*

Available from Paper Angel Press
in hardcover, trade paperback, digital, and audio editions.
paperangelpress.com